After Lucas

Stonegate Series – Book Two

Tudor Robins

Tudor Robins
www.tudorrobins.ca

Book Layout © 2017 BookDesignTemplates.com

After Lucas / Tudor Robins . -- 1st ed.
ISBN 978-0-9958887-5-3

Other Books by Tudor Robins:

Stonegate Series:

Objects in Mirror (Book One)

Island Series:

Six-Month Horse (Prequel)

Appaloosa Summer (Book One)

Wednesday Riders (Book Two)

Join Up (Book Three)

Faults (Book Four)

Downhill Series:

Fall Line

Chapter One

A gaggle of little girls wearing jodhpurs, with their long braids tied with bows, clusters around the car next to our trailer.

A man with a big voice and hearty laugh is frying an egg on the hood. "Who wants sunny side up?" he asks.

A round of giggles, and one girl says, "Over easy for me!"

Those hair bows – triple layered, in shades of pink, purple and turquoise, some with gems in the middle – make them look so sweet, but I know what those girls grow up to be like.

"Mavis!" Laney snaps her fingers at me.

"Please tell me you didn't just snap at me," I say. I'm used to riding coaches being tough, but those are top-notch coaches with full barns and waiting lists. Not you-weren't-even-here-a-year-ago coaches trying to turn an old-school Western barn into a show stable.

Laney, though, hasn't received the memo that she shouldn't look a gift horse like mine in the mouth. That the only reason we're boarding at her "up-and-coming" barn is that her brother plays on the hockey team my dad manages – that she should consider us giving her our business as a favour. That me and my ribbon-winning warmblood machine deserve a little more respect. "Please tell me you know you needed to be mounted and ring-ready five minutes ago," she answers.

And, yeah, I do know. With no groom, and next-to-no help, I'm all too aware of my schedule at this show.

When I left my last barn, I told them I was going someplace bigger, better, and shinier; somewhere I wouldn't even have to tack up my own horse.

If only that had worked out.

If I thought I was sick of showing before, well, let's just say searing sun, rock-hard footing, thirty-two degrees in the shade, and a show crew of me-myself-and-I isn't helping.

"Mavis!" Laney snaps again. "Tighten your girth, brush off your boots, and get to the ring. Now." She's already walking away as she calls, "I'll see you there in four minutes."

No. The word bubbles up in me. I'm hot. I'm tired. I'm hungry. I already have so many ribbons that I don't even bother to keep them anymore.

I squint through the sun at my mare standing next to the trailer. Even though she doesn't have a hay net, she's patient. Even though she doesn't have a decent groom, she's clean and shiny.

Maybe I should just load her on the trailer and declare our day done.

The main problem with that plan is I really have no idea how to do that. Loading Ava has always been somebody else's job. My protest will lose a lot of its impact if I have to call Laney for help halfway through.

"Wanna Timbit?"

"What?" I turn to stare at a set of cheeks, chin, and collarbone so edgy you could cut yourself on them, face so pale the skin's almost blue, sharp nose pinched like a fox's muzzle, and reddish hair reinforcing the foxy impression. Sasha.

Eleven-year-old Sasha, and her flashy paint pony, Oreo (show name Cookies 'n' Cream) are the other half of Laney's show "team." Which, I suppose, means we should be bonding.

"My mom went to Timmie's at lunch. She got a forty-pack."

"Uh, yeah. No. I'm about to ride. The last thing I need is jelly-filled deep-fried dough rolling around in my stomach."

"Sometimes being hungry makes you snappy." Sasha holds the box out and, sure enough, there's a jelly-filled perched right on the top. "This could help."

I give her a direct three-second stare and say, "Why don't you just snap off," before leading Ava off to find Laney.

* * *

"Whew! Can you believe they're not going to excuse jackets in this heat?"

The woman next to me appears to be talking to everybody and anybody in earshot as she tugs and releases her top with one hand, while using her program as a fan with the other.

I know her – know her daughter. The daughter used to be in my lesson at Stonegate and is as loud-mouthed as her mother.

There's a film of sweat across the woman's top lip as she says, "It's just criminal to make those poor girls wear dark jackets on a day like today. I hear they were cooking eggs on cars in the parking lot."

Ka-pow! Thwack! Blam! The words swim in front of my eyes, bolded and jagged, just like they appear in the geeky comics my brother loves to read.

It's ridiculously tempting to *Zap!* the woman.

"Mavis!" It's almost like a warning alarm goes off in Laney's head when my thoughts stray. "Do you know the course?" she asks.

I tear my eyes away from loud-woman with a sigh. "Yes."

"Tell me."

"What?"

"Tell me the course."

"I know it!"

Laney crosses her arms, lifts one eyebrow. I sigh again. "Oh, fine ... it's white vertical, to ..." Halfway through I'm not even sure I'm reciting the right course anymore. They're all so similar. Vertical, oxer, diagonal, line – toss those elements up and see what combination they fall in and – voila! – there's your Hunter course for this afternoon.

It must be right, though, because Laney nods, and the furrows smooth from her forehead, and she says, "OK, watch how the next few riders negotiate that outside line," before turning away to straighten Sasha's hair bows.

***

I'm on-deck, everything on Ava and me shining, course firmly implanted in my memory. I pass by the loud-mouthed woman one last time, on my way to the gate, and am just at the right spot to hear her whisper to another show-ring mom, "That's the girl I told you about – the one heading in now – she got kicked out of Stonegate."

My blood, skin, temper, rush an instant ten degrees warmer – there's nothing like a barb that comes a little too close to the truth to rocket me straight past hot, to full-on scorch level. I pull Ava into an unplanned circle and swing back by the two women. When my shadow falls across big-mouth, I lean forward. One deep breath holds the shake out of my voice as I say, "Just a word of advice – if they do excuse jackets, you might want to tell your daughter to leave hers on. I've never seen anyone sweat like her, and judges don't really go for the pit-stained look."

Then I ride Ava straight forward into a trot and into the ring.

* * *

It's my final class of the day and I'm one correct canter lead away from winning my division.

Unfortunately, it's the left canter lead, which is the only one we ever screw up.

And, yes, I acknowledge, being in contention for winning the division championship means I should never – like not ever – be sweating something as basic as a correct canter lead. If it was up to Ava we wouldn't be, but unfortunately for my horse, there's every chance of me getting in her way.

Long, long ago, the large pony I owned before I owned Ava had a genuine left lead canter issue. I told myself I sold the problem when we sold her, but the memory of that weakness has burrowed its way deep into my stupid, obsessive, not-at-all-intuitive brain and carried it forward, so I always anticipate trouble with the left lead. I try to "help" Ava with the lead, I completely confuse her, and ninety-eight per cent of the time she gets it right anyway – she's just that good.

We've walked and trotted on both reins – Ava striding even longer than she needs to with her already-long legs – making her look floaty and forward. It's one of the many things that contributed to her massive price tag, and it's paid off ever since in ribbon, after ribbon, after trophy, after medal.

She's held her head and neck perfectly, balanced me evenly on her back, and her right-lead canter was to die for.

We can't lose ... unless we take the right lead canter when the judge asks for the left.

It's coming. The rhythm of the show ring is ingrained deeply enough in me to know we've only got seconds left before the announcement of "Can-ter please. Canter!"

The judge, of course, is watching, but so are Laney and Sasha. So is loud-mouthed lady – in fact her daughter's in the ring with me. My old coach is watching too, along with a bunch of the other girls I used to show with. Everyone is quiet, polite – nobody wants to get on the wrong side of the judge by breaking horseshow etiquette – but if this was a less genteel sport, I'd expect catcalls.

The words ring through my head – "*She got kicked out of Stonegate ...*" – they make me want to win even more, and they make it even more likely I'll tense up and throw Ava off her game.

Oh, please ... we just have to get this one thing right, and nobody else can beat us.

Any second now ...

Whatever. I've been not much more than Ava's passenger through our time together – why get ambitious now?

I mentally shrug, and give up any last shreds of pride I have left, and when the command for the canter comes, I don't move at all – just let my horse respond to that word, and the timing she knows so well, and pick up a gorgeous, balanced left lead canter, and all I do is let my hips move in rhythm with her glass-smooth strides and before we even slow to a trot again, I know we've won the division.

Chapter Two

Division won. *Tick.*

Division-winning horse snug in a double-bedded stall eating a bran mash. *Tick.*

Me – dirty, smelly, dusty, tired, and sunburned – getting nose-wrinkling sideways glances as I pump twenty dollars of gas in the car. *Tick.*

Another post-show Saturday afternoon in the season that started feeling endless half-a-dozen championships ago.

The only thing distinguishing my show Saturdays are whether I come home sunburned or soaking wet. Today my nose is stinging – it'll start peeling the day after tomorrow.

At home I stumble up the driveway with my dirty show clothes on a hanger draped over one shoulder, a drawstring bag bulging with my wallet, phone, and unused sunscreen slung over the other, and various papers, two empty Diet Coke bottles, a random ribbon that got left in the car, and my house keys clutched in my hands.

I'm dancing from one foot to the other, and my unsteady hand takes three tries to unlock the door. When the door gives, I fall inside, scattering bag, recycling, and ribbons on the floor.

The crisp air-conditioning of the house only makes the combination of hot-person and hot-horse smells I'm sporting more obvious, and I have to pee so badly I don't know if I can spare the time to take my paddock boots off.

I'm shooting a stealthy look around to see if I can get away with sprinting to the powder room with my boots on, when my mom steps from the kitchen into the hall.

"So?" I know what she's asking, but my automatic reaction is to make her work for it.

"So, *what...?*" I ask. *Dumb move.* I cross one leg over the other. *Should have just answered.*

"The show, of course – how did it go?"

I shrug. "As expected. That's the third show in a row we've beaten the same girl to the division championship – I won't be surprised if she shows up to the next show with a big fat cheque and tries to buy Ava."

My mom gives a funny jerk with her head, and blinks twice, fast. "Speaking of which, we're going out for dinner."

I'm not sure why this is news she has to share with me. She and my dad usually go out for dinner at least once a week, leaving Rory and me to fend for ourselves. "Yeah, OK. Is there something you want to show me in the fridge ...?"

Her forehead creases. "What? Oh! No, we're *all* going out for dinner. The four of us."

"No." I shake my head and cross my legs the other way. "Nuh-uh. I've been up since 4:30, it's so hot I'm nearly cooked, and I'm filthy. I'm not going anywhere but into the shower, and then onto the couch."

My mom plants a hand on each hip. "It's not negotiable, Mavis. You can have your shower, then we'll take you – in an air-conditioned car, to an air-conditioned restaurant – and that's the way it's going to be."

She wins for two reasons.

One is that my mom rarely says flat-out "no." Almost never. Ninety-nine per cent of the time I can push back, but when she goes non-negotiable on me, I don't waste my time trying to negotiate.

Two is that I'm dying. My eyeballs must be turning yellow. It's all I can do to struggle out of my paddock boots and run for the bathroom. Standing and fighting is definitely not an option.

In the shower, my brain won't settle. Why the dinner for four tonight? Have I forgotten somebody's birthday? Is it my parents' anniversary? There's something else, too – something my mom said before; jumping from me talking about someone buying Ava to "Speaking of which ..." – but shampoo runs into my eyes, and by the time I've blinked, and rubbed, and cursed it out, I've lost my train of thought. It's not like I ever understand the way my mom's brain works, anyway.

I scrub at a stubborn smear of dirt on my arm and chalk up tonight's outing to an attack of parental guilt. I caught my mom and our next-door neighbour, Betty, chatting in the driveway the other day. Both had tears in their eyes over the imminent departure of Betty's son for university. "It seems like just yesterday he was running through the sprinkler with your two," Betty was saying in a shaky voice.

My mom laid her hand on Betty's arm. "I know. I can hardly believe it. They grow up so fast ..."

Cue non-negotiable family dinner. After all, this is Rory's last year of high school.

Come to think of it, I don't much like that idea either.

I shut my eyes tightly and stick my whole head under the water and quite literally drown out thoughts of my big brother moving away.

***

I was wrong. This dinner isn't about Rory, or me, or my mom. Unless you look at it in a certain way, in which case, it's actually about all of us.

My dad, you see, has just lost his job.

The job that pays for the sky-high property taxes on our house in the best school district in the city, that keeps three cars in our driveway, that has always covered my very expensive horse's very expensive board.

"... so," my dad's saying, "I'm sorry. I know it's bad news ..."

My mom moves her hand on top of his, holds it on the table. "It's not bad news, Andrew. We're all healthy. We're all fine. It's just an adjustment, that's all. I'm sure the kids will understand that."

Rory already has his eyes fixed on her, nodding his head. I'm the one she's staring at – *Mavis* will understand that, won't you *Mavis?* is what she really means – but, this time, she doesn't need to worry about me. I'm not going to make a fuss, because in the face of this bad news, all I feel is a surging, rising, bubbling flutter of relief.

Oh, wow.

I can stop.

Stop trekking out to the barn every single weekday.

Stop showing every Saturday, and Sunday, from early May until the fall.

Stop chasing the points I need to qualify for the end-of-season Championships, followed by the sumptuous, international-calibre, horse-centred, completely over-the-top Royal Agricultural Expo in November.

I'm done.

The other thing I am is hungry. Starving. Which isn't surprising, considering I won today's championship on two cups of green tea, half a Granny Smith apple, a cinnamon-raisin breakfast pita, three sticks of sugarless gum, and the aforementioned two bottles of Diet Coke.

My insides twist. How did I ever turn down that jelly-filled Timbit? I swear I could eat a dozen of them right this second.

At least I can do the next best thing.

I re-open the restaurant menu, scan the calorie count columns again, find that the Chicken Parmigiana Burger with a side of poutine contains more than my entire daily recommended calories, and when the waitress returns to our table to refill my brother's pint of Mountain Dew for the second time, I say, "Excuse me. Could you please change my order of Skinny Tuna Tacos for the Chicken Parm Delight?"

I never liked my size 26 breeches anyway. The zipper gives me a rash.

Rory gives me a look. He's ordered the Double Cheese and Bacon Angus Burger. The menu tells me it has a hundred and thirty-seven fewer calories than the Chicken Parm.

I lift an eyebrow. *Are you going to let me get away with that?* He's supposed to be the big eater around here.

"I'll change my fries for poutine," he says.

Weirdly – because it's normally quite a challenge for me to relate to other human beings – my brother's compromise of upping his order without eclipsing mine is completely satisfying to me and, from the wink he gives me, I know it is for him, too.

My stomach growls, and I sit back against the too-high, too-upright back of the booth, fold my hands on the packing-paper covered table, and pretend I'm listening to my dad give the details of his new life – our new lives – but really all I'm doing is waiting for my food.

I'd forgotten what it feels like to be this uncomplicatedly hungry.

***

"It sucks for Dad," Rory says.

My brother's right. It totally does. I can see that. I can nod when Rory says it. But I can't feel it.

Despite the two-thousand-six-hundred plus calories coursing through my system, I'm so light I might float away. It's like I've just shrugged off a weight vest I forgot I've been wearing for the last ... I don't even know how long.

I'm free! I'm finished!

As Rory's ball rebounds right into my hands, and I pass it back to him, I remember not to smile too widely though, because it does suck for my dad.

He still has a job, he explained to us, just not the high-profile, high-paying job he had as an executive on the local NHL team. He's been demoted – if he was a player, they'd call it being sent down – to manage the lower-league affiliate team. It's less money, likely a lot more work, and it's six hours away in a town called Rockingdown near the New York / Pennsylvania border.

Which means it also sucks for my mom, and for Rory, who will both really miss him.

I should be sorry for all of them. I should be in shock. A nice person – a kind, empathetic person – would be.

I'm not, though.

I'm just not.

Rory squares up, lets go, and we both watch as his ball arcs through the net.

"Maybe I should quit basketball," he says. "Do you think they'd refund my fees?"

I think the empathy skipped me and my brother got both our shares.

"No!" I grab the ball and hold it tight so he'll have to listen to me. I'm thinking a) his basketball fees are already paid b) the entire season of basketball costs less than one month's board for Ava c) my parents and I can agree on one thing – we all really, really want Rory to be able to play basketball. If I say the wrong thing, though, I won't convince him. "It would make Dad feel really guilty if you had to quit basketball because of him."

Rory cocks his head. I've got his attention. "It would make him feel way, way worse," I add.

"Hmm ..." Rory says. "OK. But what about you? Mom and Dad said you might need to sell Ava – that's *huge*. Won't that make him feel terrible too?"

Deflect. "Dad's used to feeling terrible about me." And before Rory can respond, I deflect again, in the form of a step forward and a dribble toward the net. "Bet you can't stop me!" I call over my shoulder and, thank goodness, my good-natured brother follows me, just like I wanted him to.

***

There's a weird reddish glow in my room, thanks to my mother "tidying" up my things – she's picked up the ribbon I dropped earlier and hooked it over my bedside light.

Probably not a fire hazard at all ... I reach out to move it, then stop.

The way it's hanging – the viewing angle I have from my bed – shows just two letters in stamped gold letters. **EM**. The show was at the Embrun Equestrian Park so, of course, the "EM" is the beginning of "Embrun," but for a second a flush of heat, then cold runs through me.

Em.

You see, that was my name.

I mean, my birth certificate has always read **Mavis** but for a long, long time, I was Em. Everybody called me that.

Looking at those two bright letters flashes me back to sunny days filled with round-bellied ponies. I remember riding in rubber boots, and splashing through mud. I remember slurping Slushies. I remember – a strange but distinct memory – a frog. Somebody had caught it.

I know it's not at all possible that life was perfect in my Em days, but there is an envelope of happiness that opens up when I think of them.

And then what happened? Well, my brother got sick – as in, we're-not-sure-what's-wrong / stay-in-the-hospital sick. And I went to stay with my Aunt Mavis while everyone tried to figure out what was wrong with Rory.

She was my dad's older sister; whose kids were also much older than me. The family was lovely to me while I was there, but nobody was particularly *loving*.

Aunt Mavis – not surprisingly – called me Mavis while I stayed with her. "It's time you used your proper name," she told me, and "Mavis" is the name she wrote on the form when she registered me at the school down the street from her house.

I read voraciously that year – *Anne of Green Gables*, and lots of Jane Austen – and both made the idea of rites of passage seem normal. If there was an age for girls to put their hair up, or wear their skirts long, it seemed there might also be an age for giving up nicknames.

At Christmas dinner, when my dad backed my aunt up by saying "I'm glad you're finally calling Mavis by her proper name," something crumpled in me; my childish nickname shriveling up and dying.

When I moved back home it was hard to settle again. Even though I hadn't bonded with my aunt's family, a space had formed between me and my own family.

We never re-started our abandoned Friday movie nights. We stopped camping for fear of what might happen if Rory had a seizure when we were hours from the closest hospital.

I dithered over asking everyone to call me Em again. First, I thought it might help, then I thought it was probably the most insignificant thing I could ask, and in the meantime, I started riding at Stonegate where they met me for the first time as Mavis, and I went back to school where my new teacher called me Mavis, and I never did get back to feeling like myself again, so having a name that didn't feel like mine didn't seem to matter.

But now, looking at those letters – **EM** – feeling the squeeze in my chest, I'm starting to wonder.

It's the red glow, I tell myself. It would creep anybody out. Turn off the light.

Roll over.

Go to sleep.

Chapter Three

While I spread cream cheese on a bagel in our tepid kitchen (my mom read that setting the air-conditioner at twenty-six degrees will save us all kinds of money), the radio repeats that the heat advisory remains in place, that libraries and community centres are available for those needing a cool place to go, and that splash pads are open in parks across the city.

My mom tuts as I stare into the depths of the refrigerator looking for a can of Diet Coke. "Opening the door accounts for twelve per cent of the fridge's energy use," she says.

"If you don't open the door, how are you supposed to use the fridge?" I ask.

There's a faint sheen on her skin, and when she blows at her hair, strands of it stick to her face. My mom's overheated and I just talked back to her. *Dumb move.*

She points to my bagel. "As soon as you're done that, you need to go to the barn."

Oh for ... "It's too hot, Mom."

"I doubt Ava agrees."

"I think Ava would very much agree. I'm sure I'm the last person she wants to see on the hottest afternoon of the summer."

I imagine the mare's dark coat hot to the touch, and the soles of my paddock boots warmed through by the sky-high temperature of the sand in the ring.

Now my mom's got the fridge door open, and is rummaging around inside. I think of repeating her energy loss stats back at her, but quickly think better of it. She emerges from the cool of the refrigerator holding a bag of carrots that have seen better days. "There, now Ava will want to see you."

Before I can protest, she continues, "Come on, Mavis. You know Ava has to be fit and schooled if we're going to get the price we want for her ..." and, before she's even done speaking that lifting airiness fills me again – *Oh, yeah ...* I'm nearly done. This is it. I'm going to post Ava for sale, and I'm going to be free.

I hold my hands out for the carrots and remember just in time not to smile too widely. Force a sigh. "OK, I guess. Fine. I'll go."

***

Once at the barn I transition into auto-pilot. I yank Ava out of the relative cool of her dark stall and stick her on cross ties. I circle the jelly scrubber over her sensitive skin – "Manners!" I warn when she twitches. Flick the resulting fine film off with a soft brush – "Hold still!" Then, even though I know there will be nothing in her whistle-clean hooves I risk back spasms and pick out her feet. Her weight shifts, and I warn her with a growl, "Don't even think about it."

Saddle and bridle neatly buckled in place, I lead the mare outside into the high, hot sun.

There's not a hint of shade in the sand ring, and not a lick of a breeze ruffling through the stable yard.

It would be cooler in the woods. Lots of people ride to the pond in weather like this.

But almost-perfect Ava does have one tiny flaw – she hates deer. More accurately, deer scare her witless. Since there's an abundance of deer in the property surrounding the stable, hacking isn't something we do very often, and when we do, I don't exactly enjoy riding my high-alert horse through trails, waiting to be carted along on a headlong bolt after coming face-to-face with a horse-eating deer.

And my riding boots and saddle are way too expensive to take into any muddy pond.

So, we ride in the sand ring.

If we had something to work on, maybe the ride would be less deadly dull, but the reality is Ava learned all she needed to know long before I owned her. Whatever I do today will make no difference to the way she goes for any potential owners. I could sit on her backwards. I could put a Western saddle on her. Honestly, I could have stayed at home in our cool house, and left her in her cool stall, and she would impress any prospective buyer who deigns to settle their seat bones onto her responsive back.

It's just what she does. Performs like a pro. Even with a poseur like me on her back.

Because I have no idea what else to do I work through a checklist of "things we already know how to do," which is boring, but failsafe ... until Ava misses a flying change on her left lead. Quite obviously this has to be my fault because Ava is flying-change-perfect, and only a truly terrible sequence of aids would cause her to miss a lead change, but the more I try to fix it, the worse it gets.

Only an idiot would pursue mid-afternoon canter work under a cloudless summer sky, and I am that idiot.

"It's too hot to ride."

Cutting through the body heat and sweat – horse and human – and the flush mounting in my head and on my cheeks, comes the icy-sharp little voice.

My head snaps to the fence. Fox-Girl.

"What?" I say.

"I wanted to ride, but my mom told me it was too hot."

Between the jelly-filled Timbits, and the basic common sense, I'm starting to think I like Sasha's mom more than I like my own.

I grunt. "Yeah? Well my mom kicked me out of the house to come ride."

"Hmm ... well, she looks pretty hot."

I glance down at Ava's neck. I hadn't realized just how sweaty she was. There are twin lines of foam outlining the path of the reins against her coat.

I reach out and, sure enough, I feel the heat a good six inches before I even touch her soaked-through coat.

Shit.

She's far too hot.

Crap.

Panic rushes me. Oh, God, what happens to a horse that overheats? Will she colic? Will she die? I'll be in so much trouble if, instead of selling Ava for a profit, we have to pay for the vet to come and euthanize her.

I jump off and run my stirrups up in record time. Undo the girth and lift the saddle off and there isn't even a darker area under the saddle pad – Ava's completely wet all over. The saddle pad is a hot, sweaty, disgusting mass.

"Laney was looking for you."

"What?" I'd forgotten about Fox-Girl.

"I saw her in the office. She said she was going to come and find you to tell you something."

I watch Ava's heaving sides.

"There's foam between her hind legs." Sasha might think that's helpful news. I don't.

Especially not when Laney could be here any second. Standing as far back as the reins will let me, and looking at my mare, she looks exhausted. Head low, sides rising and falling, and not one patch of dry coat.

Oh, God-Oh, God-Oh, God ...

There's only one thing to do.

I gather the reins and start walking. The normally perfectly mannered Ava, who always walks forward, at my shoulder, drags behind me. "Come on, come on, come on ..." *Tug, yank, pull.*

"Where are you going?" Sasha's voice follows us.

"To the duck pond," I say.

It's my only hope. When Laney sees Ava, she needs to believe her head-to-toe soaking is due to water. The pond is the fastest way I can think to accomplish that. Especially because the pond's in the opposite direction from Laney's office, so heading there should buy me a little more time.

Sasha claps. "Oh, that's fun! A swim! Maybe I should get Oreo!"

No way. I cannot babysit this girl and her pony. "Maybe you should get me her halter and a lead shank instead?" I suggest. "If you bring them to the pond, I'll switch them for her bridle."

"Oh! OK!"

"And, you could take the saddle into the tack room and put it on the rack for me to clean."

"I guess ... if it would help."

Smile, Mavis. Be nice. "It would be a big help!" I say.

"OK!" I'll see you there soon.

And that is how it happens that when Laney finds me, I am personifying the idyllic, peaceful, girl-and-horse-in-the-summer image that ends up as the background for syrupy memes on social media.

You know the ones that say There's nothing so good for the inside of a person as the outside of a horse or To ride on a horse is to fly without wings or Ride your troubles away.

That's me and Ava right now – sun sparkling off the pond's surface, Ava in cool-but-not-cold water that comes halfway up her barrel, nobody hot, nobody sweating, everybody just chilling on a hot summer afternoon.

"Don't you two look happy? I should take a picture for her sale posting," Laney says.

I uncross my fingers, unclench my jaw. Thank goodness for Ava's high level of fitness, and her general good nature – she's snapped back to calm, cool, and collected very quickly.

"Not that we need more pictures," Laney's saying. "My sister's neighbour's daughter saw Ava's posting, and she's so in love with her she's driving from Kingston tomorrow to try her."

"Wow," I say. "Kingston. She sounds motivated."

"Well, she's definitely interested. They'll leave straight from school; they're hoping to get here around five."

I nod. "I can be here."

"Alright. That's good." Laney takes a couple of steps away, then turns back. "Just do me a favour and don't ride the hell out of your horse before Laurel gets here tomorrow? Especially if it's thirty degrees again. It would be nice if she had all her energy."

What? How did she know? Did Sasha tell her?

I open my mouth, but asking any of those questions isn't going to help my cause, so I clamp it closed again. Laney's already walking away, so I content myself with sticking my tongue out at her retreating back. Then, when Sasha runs up, panting, holding out Ava's halter, I ask her, "What did you do? Stop for ice cream on the way?"

And in that way, I feel, if not exactly *better*, at least normal again.

Chapter Four

I pull the car as far forward and as much to the left of the driveway as I can. It's a habit, to leave the area around the basketball net free for Rory. As long as it's not snowing – even the odd day when it is, but there's no actual accumulation on the ground – Rory shoots fifty free throws. At least.

He stands now, ball on hip, watching me park with the bumper almost touching his bike leaned against the garage door.

"Wanna shoot hoops?" he asks.

I look down at my dirt-streaked breeches and my sweat-stained shirt. Hunger pangs clench my stomach. I have this all-over feeling of grime that will only be dispelled by a skin-reddeningly hot shower.

"Yes." I say.

I have to, because of the promise I made the last time Rory had a seizure. *Just stop*, I begged the cosmos, or Mother Nature, or whoever's in control of these things. *No more seizures.* Please. I won't ask for anything else. Nothing for me. Just this, for Rory. You do this for him, and I'll do anything I can. I swear.

So, every single day Rory is motivated enough, and pumped enough, and healthy enough to shoot hoops – and every single time he asks me to join him – I say yes.

I don't even think about it. It's yes. Yes. Yes.

He bounce-passes me the ball and, as I square up to take the shot my stomach grumbles long and loud.

"You're hungry," he says.

"Yup." I nod. "Don't worry – I'll still be hungry after I beat you to ten in free throws."

"You are so on," he says.

"Yes I am." I release the ball, follow its trajectory with my hands, pointing it through the air and into the basket. Laugh as it swishes through, and add, "Unfortunately for you."

***

My mom comes into the kitchen as I'm perfecting the shocking orange cheese-like paste in the saucepan, ready to dump in the noodles for my near-nightly Kraft Dinner feast.

She lifts her eyebrows at yet another dinner of unnaturally coloured-and-flavoured, highly salted and processed boxed food but I heard her talking to my aunt on the phone – telling her it's a step up from earlier in the summer when my usual dinner was nothing-at-all – so she just taps the refrigerator door and says, "There are some steamed vegetables left over from when Rory and I ate earlier, if you'd like those ...?"

"Thanks, no." I gesture to the ketchup bottle on the counter. "Vegetables in a bottle. Perfect for me."

She wrinkles her nose and I can almost see her thinking she'll solve this problem by just not buying any more KD, which makes me decide to throw her a bone.

"Laney says there's a very motivated buyer coming to try Ava tomorrow."

When my mom lifts her eyebrows that high, all the wrinkles smooth out of her face. "Really? How motivated?"

I add a dab more milk – skim milk so, see? My dinner's not that unhealthy – and the sauce is nearly smooth enough. "She's driving from Kingston."

"Kingston," she mutters. "That sounds serious."

A stray noodle has escaped and I pop it into the saucepan. "Serious buyers are usually the best kind."

My mom sighs. "Are you sure you're OK with this, Mavis? I mean, it feels like I'm more upset about having to sell Ava than you are."

I dig the spatula deep under the pasta so I can pull the cheese up and make sure it's evenly distributed. "Let's be realistic, Mom. Her monthly board is the equivalent of an entire extra mortgage payment – am I right?"

She nods.

"Can we afford an entire extra mortgage payment right now?"

She shakes her head.

I shrug. "So, she's gotta go. And, with the results we've had over the past year, and her being rock-solid sound, she should actually be worth more than when we bought her." I don't mention that a lesser horse than Ava might not have stayed so sound after the way I overrode her today. "It's a rare financial win in the horse world."

This was the smart approach. My mom can't argue with the financial logic, so I don't have to elaborate. Don't have to explain my absolute absence of any feeling at all when I set eyes on Ava. Don't have to confront my fear that if I can't love such a perfect horse, there's something very wrong with me. Like, possibly, I'm secretly a robot. I also don't have to admit that I know everybody talks about me behind my back – says Ava and I only win ribbons because of Ava's skills – and that I can't confront them because it's the absolute truth.

I have to give my mom a little credit, though, because she does push – a bit. "What are you going to do without her, though, Mavis? Going to the barn has been your life."

Life. That's just it. I'm going to have a life again. The balloon of happiness rises in me again.

I'm going to eat a lot of Kraft Dinner at more reasonable hours. I'm going to grow my fingernails, and they won't always have dirt under them. Maybe I'll get a part-time job and save some money in case things go completely tits-up with Dad's job – that way at least I'll be able to buy groceries for Rory and me. Maybe – here's a thought – maybe I'll make a friend, or two, who doesn't ride horses, and doesn't secretly want me to rise on the wrong diagonal, or for Ava to rub her braids out, so she can beat me in the big class of the day.

"I thought you needed me to drive Rory to basketball while you're working."

Another good tactical manoeuvre. The gist of the "things are going to change around here" speech we got at the restaurant was that a) my dad has to move away, b) we can't afford to keep Ava c) after nearly twenty years at home my mom is going to go start work after Labour Day d) I'll need to pick up most of the driving duties for Rory's basketball.

I'm so glad there hasn't been any discussion of Rory quitting basketball – I'm cool with him shouldering as little as possible of the fall-out of my dad's career shift. I figure the not-fully-understood seizure disorder my brother's grown up with, which means he still hasn't been able to get his driver's license even though he's a year older than me, and which hangs over him like a rain-laden thundercloud every day of his life, is enough for him to be getting on with.

My mom blinks twice. "Well, yes, I do ..."

"And that's how many times a week?" I ask.

"Um, well, of course it will depend on the schedule."

"It sounds to me like even if we didn't need the money we'd have to sell Ava just so I'd have time for all that driving."

My mom double-blinks again. My KD's getting cold. Time to bring this conversation to a close. "I'm hungry."

Magic words. Even though I'm not eating what she wishes I would, at least I want to eat.

"Oh, of course. Eat it before it gets cold."

I shove in a mouthful of cheesy noodles. Nod. *Will do.*

***

I'm reviewing Ava's "For Sale" posting on the "Horses 613" forum. I'm pretty proud of it. I went through all the postings for the last few weeks and made a list of the most popular descriptors being used, then I tried to use them all in Ava's ad.

- Pins in every class
- Point and shoot
- Extensive show mileage
- Auto changes
- No spook, no stop, no vices
- Unparalleled ground and traveling manners
- Never marish
- UTD on farrier, vet, teeth

Now I'm wondering if I should add, High level of resiliency despite inane moves by inept owner.

The headlights of my dad's car strobe through my open bedroom windows. Bright, then gone. The engine cuts. Wait ... wait ... wait ... the front door opens, then shuts.

The murmur of my mom's voice – I bet you anything she's offering him those steamed vegetables from earlier – and he must say yes because I can't hear them anymore, meaning they've left the hall for the kitchen.

When I look back at my laptop screen it's frozen; the little blue wheel spinning and spinning. It's as done with this posting as I am.

I stand, stretch, and head for the bathroom.

Through the slice of his not-quite-closed door I can see Rory sprawled on his bed. He's got his laptop open with an Excel spreadsheet up. Basketball stats. He loves them. He finds, reads, analyzes, collects, and organizes stats. When he was younger it was dinosaurs – he could tell you weight, height, territory range, period they were alive on earth; you name it. Then there was Pokemon and, let me tell you, the stats associated with Pokemon are as abundant as they are baffling. Now, as much as I know he enjoys the physical aspect of the game, I think it's the never-ending supply of stats that cements basketball as his favourite pastime. Even when he went through a particularly bad period with his seizures – when he couldn't even play on a house team, never mind competitive – he pored over stats.

I think they kept him sane, so even though I call him a weirdo to his face, watching him deep in statistical concentration makes a smile flit across my face.

I lock the bathroom door behind me and barefoot across the room, sink to my seat bones on the cool tile floor, and listen. There's a vent here, and if my parents are saying anything at all in the kitchen, their voices will float up through it.

The first thing I hear is "Thank you. I was hungry."

It's quiet for a few seconds then my mom's voice, sounding small, sounding strangled, says. "I'm going to miss you."

The bursts of my secret floating happiness haven't left me the space or inclination to identify with my mom's feelings about my dad's move. A band tightens across my throat as my dad says, "We'll figure it out."

"I'm worried," my mom says.

"Sit down and tell me."

She talks for a few minutes about how it's been such a long time since she's worked, and how it will be a big adjustment and, also, is going into business with a friend a good idea? And my dad says a lot of "It'll be OK," and

"You'll do fine once you adjust," and "You're smarter than you think," and "You might actually find out you really like it."

I've splayed my legs in a wide "V" to get more of the cooling effect of the tiles, and there's a breeze floating down from the open window above my head, and for the first time in the long, hot, day I'm feeling relaxed and not-sweaty, and that's when I hear it – "Mavis" – it snaps me to attention.

"I just can't read her."

My dad makes a snorting sound. "That's nothing new."

"I know, but this time ... I thought she'd at least resist when we said Ava had to be sold. I thought she'd still want to ride a couple of times a week – even if it was just in lessons. So, I figured we'd let her use the car for that in exchange for her driving Rory – but she just seems not to care, about anything ..."

"So?" my dad prompts.

"So, I don't have any leverage. I can only *ask* her to drive – I can't force her. She could walk away at any time, and then what?"

I'm not relaxed anymore. I lift my knees to my chest and pull them in tight with my left arm. *How can she?* I want to run downstairs and yell, 'How can you even suggest I'd ever leave Rory high and dry? How awful do you think I am?'

But a) I'm not ready to let them know about my secret eavesdropping place and b) my aunt, who's a trial lawyer, once told me "Never ask a question you don't already know the answer to." I'm not ready to ask my mom how low her opinion is of me. I'm not confident what her answer would be, and I'm not sure I could handle it.

Instead I scramble to my feet, stretching cold stiffness out of my leg muscles, shaking the pins and needles out of the right hand I had curled at an awkward angle under me.

On my way back to my room, I stick my head in Rory's door. "Hey," I say.

"Yeah?"

"Did I hear you're registered for try-outs?"

"Uh-huh."

"First session next week?"

"Yup."

"I'm driving you."

He nods. "That's the word on the street."

"Just checking to make sure you're not going to embarrass me. You'd better work on your free throws between now and then. I'm not driving and having you not make the team."

"Just so we're clear it's all about you?"

"Definitely. All about me."

"Do you want me to go out and shoot some hoops now?" He points at the glaring dark square that forms his bedroom window.

I wrinkle my nose. Pretend to consider it. "Tomorrow morning will do." I take one step back. "First thing, though."

Chapter Five

The girl looks great on my horse. My horse looks great under her. Which shouldn't come as a surprise considering that's what Ava's always been about; making her rider look amazing. When I bought her, I wasn't looking for potential, or a project. I didn't want to build a relationship. I wanted to win ribbons. Which I have, steadily, so many that when I look at them now I don't even care anymore.

It's time for me – Ava – us, to move on.

I watch for the canter aid the girl gives Ava, but I can't spy even a hint of leg movement. My mare just steps sweetly forward into a rocking horse canter on the left lead – of course she does – and, *chink*, an extra brick slots into place on my bitterness wall.

"She's going to buy her." How is this foxy little girl always in the wrong place, at the wrong time?

"That's the idea," I say.

"Well, yeah, but she's your horse. Didn't anyone ever tell you you're supposed to love your horse?"

"Didn't anyone ever tell you kids like you should be seen and not heard?"

Sasha sticks her tongue out, and even it has a vulpine point to it, then she darts off just as Laney leans in next to me.

"Ava's going well."

And the award for stating-the-obvious goes to Laney Williams.

Here's the thing, though – I like Laney. I like how she's smart, and she tells the truth without being mean about it and, yes, I probably like her a bit because she's quite beautiful and while I don't always feel human, even I can't escape the biological tendency to be attracted to attractive people. I don't hate Laney so I don't call her out on her inane comment.

"She's a good rider." My turn to state the obvious.

Laney lays her hand, warm-and-dry, on my arm. How does she do that? My palms are always freezing cold, or sweaty – it's why I try to avoid touching human beings with them; stick to horses – and she says, "I know this has to be difficult for you, Mavis, but I can't think of a better place for her to go."

I can't either. This is Ava's lucky day. Going to the beautiful countryside near Kingston to be pampered in a snug barn – they actually showed me pictures – with a rider who will never confuse her with ambiguous aids, never reef her in the mouth on the landing of a jump, never complete an entire circuit of the ring posting on the wrong diagonal. Ava is going from surviving to living.

She deserves it. She's a good horse.

My eyes tingle. If only Fox Girl could see me now – it's possible I'm on the verge of shedding a tear.

Except, I *am* trying to sell Ava, and I am glad of it. The girl's mother is walking toward us. As soon as she's a little closer, I'm going to raise my voice and tell Laney I see a real connection between Ava and the girl – it's a trick I've learned from the sale boards; people always want to believe there's some sort of it-was-meant-to-be bond between them and the horse they're trying.

I'm opening my mouth when my chance to say anything at all is cut off by a ringing whinny from the small square-logged, wood-chinked annex barn less than a hundred metres from the ring.

"Oh! Lucas!" Laney says.

"Who? What?"

"A new horse," Laney says. "He just arrived today, and I thought he was settling OK, but maybe not."

Judging from the second, and third deafening whinnies that followed the first, it seems like she's right.

Most riders simply ignore the occasional whinny, but this guy is so loud that the girl trying Ava has stopped and is staring toward the barn. Her mother is, as well.

"Oh ..." Laney says. "Not good. Do. Not. Distract. The. Buyers." She looks around. "Maybe Sasha can go see what's bothering him. Where's she gone?"

But if Fox-Girl has the uncanny ability to always be where I don't want her, she's also quite good at not being around when I could really use her. She's nowhere in sight.

It's pretty clear nobody can concentrate on anything while the unseen horse is setting up such a ruckus. In other words, the girl in the ring can't concentrate on buying my horse.

"I'll go."

Laney whirls to me. "Really? That would be great ... I mean if you don't mind ... I'll give them the heavy sell on Ava while you're gone."

Let's face it, Laney is both more likeable and more knowledgeable than me. And she's the one with the connection to these people. If either of us should stay, it's her.

"No, I don't mind. It's good. I'll go."

As I walk, I call out, "OK, OK. I'm coming. Pipe down!"

The whinnying pauses, and I say, "That's better," and am immediately answered by a throaty whicker rumbling through the nearest window.

I step to the door of the barn, and as my eyes adjust from the bright sunshine of outdoors, I hear the rustling of bedding inside, then a big face, adorned with a broad white blaze, appears in the stall door.

"What is up with you?" I ask.

He whickers again.

No horse has ever whickered for me. Ever. I've always rolled my eyes when I've heard other girls at the barn saying, "Did you hear that? He whickered for me."

Yeah, right. Horses whicker for food. I'm bad-tempered but even I've been known to make nice noises when my brother opens a bag of caramel popcorn.

I always told myself Ava didn't whicker for me because I didn't spoil her with treats.

I've never seen this horse before, and I've certainly never given him a carrot, or apple, or lump of sugar – not even a flake of hay – but that deep nicker was definitely for me.

I take one step into the barn. "Shit, dude, I'm touched."

His face, now that my eyes have adjusted, is a nice chestnut colour, and would probably be pretty if it wasn't topped by a burr-entwined forelock. Like people who say all babies look the same, I've always secretly thought all horses look the same – expression-wise, anyway – even if I'd never tell a horse-crazy person so, I've never believed a horse can look happy, or sad, or surprised. I swear this one looks intensely curious, though.

I move within his reach and he sniffs me all over – nostrils flaring, traveling his muzzle up one arm, across my face, and down the other. "Jeez, Dude," I say. "Ever heard of personal space?"

He snorts, a long rattling breath that dampens my skin. "Charming," I say. "Now listen, we're trying to sell a horse here, so you need to shut up. Capiche?"

I swear he nods. In reality I think I really, really want him to nod, and I imagine it, because as soon as I step back out of the barn he shoves his head out over the bars, takes a deep breath, and gives that bellowing whinny again – nostrils flaring, sides vibrating.

Everyone in the ring turns to look, again. I shrug and keep walking, and he does it again. Laney's glare is clear – *Fix it.*

How? I suppose I could throw him a flake of hay but I've never set foot in this barn before, and don't know where the hay is stored and, also, I'm not even sure whether he can, or should, have hay.

He's still bellowing, though, so I turn on my heel, and head back to the demanding gelding, who immediately heaves a big sigh, and shuts up.

"Really?" I ask. "You've got to learn to hold out for something bigger than the company of a random stranger. If you were loud enough I would totally have had to find some food for you."

He exhales a long, loud, rattling breath and presses his face against my arm and I discover if I stand in just the right spot, the angle's right that I can see out to the sand ring and watch a new rider fall in love with my old horse. So, I do that, and while I do I pull the burrs out of the stocky chestnut's forehead and tell him, "They're probably better off without me."

He just sighs, and lowers his head as though to say, 'Don't miss the burr right up top there,' and I obediently work it out.

Chapter Six

We're all at the airport in our uniforms.

My brother, straight from a pre-try-out pick-up basketball session, is all broad shoulders and long legs in his baggy basketball shorts and **Shooting Stars** jersey.

There's a Tim Horton's kiosk across the way and he's watching a young boy and girl walking away – more accurately he's eyeing the crullers they're biting into.

My mother is busy-mom-of-teenagers. She's carrying a huge bag that obviously has anything needed to respond to any of life's emergencies, and her light blue capris, and matching light-blue-and-white striped top show she has it all together.

She points at the departures board. "On time," she says. There's a shake in her voice. I don't think she's relishing single parenting us. Or, possibly, me.

My dad has a leather bag slung over his shoulder, and another boxy black suitcase on wheels. The khaki pants and white button-down he's wearing for this evening flight where most other people have on shorts, or jeans, or yoga pants, tell everyone that in real life – during the day – he obviously wears a suit.

He's head down, swiping the screen of his phone. Important.

I get the most looks. Tall black boots, breeches, a fitted polo shirt made of special wicking fabric. Good thing most of the looks are quick, though, because on closer inspection my boots are dusty, the breeches smeared. My shirt is wet under the arms, and the only reason I'm wearing my **Spruce Meadows** ballcap is because of the ferocity of my helmet hair.

Also, my size twenty-six breeches, which used to be baggy, are definitely form-fitting now.

I used to be a good fake – true I never was a proficient rider – but I got whip-thin, and kept my boots polished, and won championships, and looked the part.

Now Ava's on her way out of my life – loaded into the Kingston-bound trailer for a two-week-long trial. And me? Well I guess I can go home, and chuck these clothes in the laundry, and never wear them again.

A little girl walks by, wheeling a pink and purple Barbie Princess bag while she tugs at her mom's sleeve and points at me. "... horse ..." I hear her say.

I should smile at her but I can't. *Don't look at me, honey, your Barbie probably rides her Barbie horse better than I've ridden my mare for the last couple of years.*

At least I'm not the only fake. Nobody watching the four of us together, seeing my dad off, would know the carefully orchestrated dinner where he told us he was leaving was the last time, before this, all four of us were in the same room.

We're not a close family, but we play one on my mom's Facebook timeline, and in our yearly Christmas cards, and here – watching my dad board a plane for his new bachelor apartment in the hinterland of southern New York state.

We cluster at the entrance to the security area. The corrals formed of lengths of retractable webbing are empty for this mid-week evening flight, but the powers that be aren't about to take them down. Meaning my dad will have to zig and zag, weave and loop back on himself to get to the opening beyond which are the big machines and the bins for dumping belts, and shoes, and electronics.

"Bye," my mom says as she hugs him, and my dad smooths her hair and says, "You'll do fine," and, "As soon as I get settled you can come spend a couple of days," and "We'll talk every day."

"See ya!" my brother says, and he and my dad do a kind of bear-hug, arm-punch thing. "I'll miss you kiddo," my dad says, "But maybe you can visit and we'll go to a Syracuse game."

"That would be cool," Rory says, with his eyes still sliding toward the Tim Horton's. I envy my brother the simplicity of knowing exactly what he wants.

My turn. My awkward, graceless turn to say good-bye. "So, uh, bye." I say. Everything in me tightens as I step in for my hug and I make it quick. "Sorry, my shirt's dirty," I say.

"It's OK," my dad says, but he brushes at his breast pocket. "Will you be OK?" he asks. "You know, with everything that's going on with riding, and Ava?"

I shrug. "It is what it is." I could let him off the hook of this last-minute guilt he's feeling. Could tell him that his new job, us having less money, Ava going up for sale, forced some decisions I didn't have the initiative, or guts to make on my own. But I won't do that. I need to hold some ammo. Being hard done by might come in handy at some point, so I shrug again, "What are you gonna do?"

It's true I haven't reacted the way they probably expected me to: throwing a hissy fit. Yelling and crying about my horse being sold. Accusing them of ruining my life.

But I haven't tried to ease things for them either.

I haven't been kind.

The terrible catch twenty-two is that when I'm unhappy with myself, I can't find the energy to be kind to other people and now, the promising glimmer of happy hope I've been feeling deep inside me, comes from a development that's humiliating and stressing my dad, leaving my mom worried and lonely, and depriving my brother of the father he loves to talk sports with.

So, I can't be nice when I'm unhappy, and I'm mostly made happy by other people's unhappiness.

When I think of it that way, it's no surprise I don't have friends – even I have trouble liking myself.

Chapter Seven

I'm not sure what happened to soaring freedom, and my time being my own, and an end to smelling of horse all the time – I'm walking out of a barn and I definitely smell like horse.

Actually, I'm more like scuttling – as much as it's possible to scuttle when weighed down by twenty-seven kilograms of horse *stuff*.

The call came this morning, from Drew, my old coach at Stonegate, informing me they'd just discovered a Rubbermaid in the storage loft with Ava's name Sharpied on it. My mind flitted back to the bright, hot day when I'd loaded Ava into the trailer for the trip away from Stonegate. The last thing on my mind that day were Thinsulate turnout blankets and detachable neck protectors. But that's what Drew's found – Ava's bin full of winter stuff.

"Oh," I'd said. "OK, I guess I'll come and get it."

"If you would," Drew said. "The barn's very full these days, and we need all the space we can get."

Great. The other thing I remember about that day Ava and I left Stonegate for good, is the way I talked to Grace.

High and mighty. Like I'd been solicited by Her Majesty's equestrian representative to move my horse to the stables at Windsor Palace.

My experience at the Embrun horse show tells me that lie didn't get much traction.

But that bin is full of a lot of expensive gear. I can't just leave it.

I get in the car right away, in the hopes of hitting the barn at a mostly empty time of day, and cross my fingers that, at least, everything was washed before I dumped it in the Rubbermaid in the spring.

It wasn't. There's no way the gigantic bin will fit in the hatch of the tiny, eye-aching blue economy car my mom got as a cheap trade-in for the sleek black SUV that used to be our second car. The minute I open the lid to unload it, I'm hit with the stench of sweat, rain, snow, horse, dirt, and definitely some manure, all sealed in a more-or-less airless environment in soaring summer temperatures.

Wow. Suddenly perfect little Ava doesn't seem so sweet anymore.

Once I unpack the blankets, my winter riding boots, and the assorted other gear, the compact trunk is jammed. There's no way the actual Rubbermaid is fitting back there.

It's a good bin. Hardly used. Not a mark on it. I leave it neatly beside the spot where I parked my car. *There*. It's my contribution to the barn. Never let it be said I'm not generous. Plus, Drew will know I came to pick up my stuff.

I'm just about to leave the wide parking area and enter the long, tree-lined driveway, when a figure steps in front of me – since I'm obeying the 15 km / h posted speed limit there's no way I can avoid stopping.

It's Drew. I roll down the window.

"Mavis." My heart does a weird tripping thing and hammers against my ribs – I'm convinced he knows I ditched the Rubbermaid in the parking spot and he's going to give me hell.

"Yes," I say. "Hi. I got the stuff."

"Thank you."

I'm sure, "You're welcome," should mark the end of this conversation, but he's still leaning on my car.

"I hear Ava is for sale," he says.

"Oh. Yes. She's actually out on trial."

He nods. "I'm not surprised. She's a great horse." He doesn't have to add, *Who masked what a poor rider you are.* I hear the unspoken words.

"Hard to argue with that."

"You look well," he says. My mom's used the same code a couple of times lately. It means "You've gained weight," but it's meant not to panic me back into starving myself again. I flashback to the little sit-down Drew had with me

– the one that made me sure he was about to kick me out – when he told me I was too thin, and something needed to change. In light of that, this comment from Drew also means, "I was right. I told you so."

Back off. My jaw's clenched so tightly, I'm only able to make a kind of, "Hmm ..." noise in response.

I put the car in gear. *Hint, hint,* but he shifts his weight and asks, "So, if Ava's on trial, are you riding?"

An image of the crazy whinnying chestnut gelding flashes into my head. "There's a horse."

Even as my outer voice says the words, my inner voice is protesting, *Major bullshit alert!* Hinting I have a horse to ride, because I spent five minutes detangling the gelding's forelock, is like somebody asking me if I have a boyfriend, and saying, "There's a guy ..." because I said "Thank you" to the sandwich artist who made my lunch at Subway.

Whatever. Why does it matter if I lie to Drew? After this, there really should never be any reason for me to see him again.

"Good." He straightens, and taps the roof of the car. "It's important to stay in the saddle. I suppose I'll see you around the circuit, then."

"Probably!" I say. *Not if I see you first,* I think.

I accelerate away thinking that truly is *it*. No more need to go to stables. No more need to drive around in cars that smell like – I wrinkle up my nose – well, like this one does right now.

Which makes it weird when I haven't even reached the highway and I'm already thinking about the very-loud Lucas again. Teasing the burrs out of his mane should have made him look better, but the end result reminded me of a picture I saw of my mom on her way to her high school prom. "What is up with your hair?" I'd asked of the kinky, frizzy, mess bouffonning from her head. "It was a home perm," she said. "Everyone had them."

Thinking of Lucas with his comical home-perm forelock makes me smile.

Until I stop to turn onto the highway and the still air of the car thickens again with that pungent sweaty-dirty-poopy odour. What am I going to do with a trunkful of equipment for a horse I don't even physically have anymore?

That wipes the smile off my face.

Chapter Eight

When I get home my progress into the driveway is blocked by two lanky guys swishing basketballs through the net at the curb.

I stop. Stare. Wait. Stare some more.

If Rory's trying to piss me off – well, he might be succeeding secretly but I'm never going to let him know.

If he's trying to make me lose my cool, honk the horn, rev the engine, then he's going to lose.

I cut the engine, leave the car where it is – not exactly *parked* in the strict definition of wheels-in-alignment-six-inches-from-the-curb, but stationary and not likely to get hit on our quiet residential street – and walk a wide detour around my brother's spray-painted basketball key.

Back straight. Look cool. No eye contact.

"Hey!"

Don't look.

"Sis!"

Don't answer.

"You can't leave the car there!"

Do. Not. Turn. Around. "I think I just did!"

On the front step I do turn around, quickly, just enough to see my brother right back at it; shooting the ball, lunging for the rebound, but not in time to keep it from bouncing off the hood of the car. His friend is stopped, standing, holding his ball, looking at me.

I don't recognize him. While Rory was unable to play basketball, he concentrated his efforts on his alternative loves – immersing himself in clubs like Robotics, Advanced Lego, Tech and, of course, anything to do with data or stats. You can call it stereotyping, but I just call it the truth; it meant most of the friends he's been hanging out with the last couple of years are short and skinny with bad haircuts and worse fashion sense. The guy on our driveway is at least not short. From here he looks like he might have a muscle or two, and his hair, at a hundred paces, appears somewhat normal.

Which doesn't mean anything. He's still hanging out with my brother, which means even though he has an athletic physique there's probably still something really weird about him.

Whatever. At least Rory has friends. I do, sometimes, envy him the easy, accepting camaraderie of his band of robotics-squad, coding-club pals, but I'd never tell him that.

Instead, when he brings them home for lunch, I shove their shoes aside, take their food out of the microwave to put mine in, and give them the evil eye if they get in my way. Rory's new friend might as well get used to the drill so I shoot him my best scowl / frown / glare and step through the door.

The phone's ringing as I get inside. Which is fine – I know how to deal with that – wait long enough and it'll stop.

See? There. Stopped. I bend down to untie my paddock boot laces and it immediately starts ringing again.

"Oh, for God's ..." I mutter under my breath, then "Hello?"

"Mavis. We do not answer the phone in that tone of voice."

"It's the tone of voice I use to answer the phone."

"Not in my house."

I just did, Mom. I bite my tongue, though. I'm already bored of this conversation. "What is it, Mom?"

"I tried your cell phone half-a-dozen times. Why didn't you answer?"

My phone. Shit. The thing is, I've lost my phone. Again. Actually, to be fair, the last time I didn't lose it – I dropped it in Ava's stall and she stepped on it – but the effect was the same; my mom went ballistic and threatened to make me pay for a new phone until she realized she's the one who really wants me to have a phone – especially now that she needs me to be on call to drive Rory around – so she bought me another one which, yeah, I now can't remember seeing for several days.

"I was at the barn. And then I was driving. I don't answer the phone when I do either of those things."

"Mavis, please tell me you haven't lost your phone again."

"I had to drive all the way to Stonegate." It's a Hail Mary pass – the equivalent of my dad saying, "Look, Rory! A Tyrannosaurus!" when Rory was four and my dad wanted to distract him to steal half the French fries off his plate.

It works. "Stonegate? Why?"

"Drew summoned me out to pick up a heap of Ava's winter stuff that was still there."

"Oh ..." There's something wistful in my mom's voice. Like most riding moms, she had a soft spot for Drew. He's very good at making cheque-writing clients feel special. I guess it's just hitting her that the events of the last little while – moving from Stonegate, selling Ava – mean our family is even less special than we used to be. She rallies quickly, though, and her next sentence comes out no-nonsense with an edge of stress; the mother I recognize. "Well, it's just as well you're back. Have you talked to Rory yet?"

"I ... uh ..." I squint through the glass panel beside the door in time to see my brother and his new buddy collide mid-air. Rory spills onto the pavement, and the new guy reaches out his hand, pulls him to his feet. "No. Not really."

"Well, he needs to be at basketball try-outs in ..." During the pause, I can picture her shooting her hand out in front of her so her watch clears her sleeve. "... forty minutes."

"What? No. His first try-out is tomorrow."

"It *was* tomorrow, but there was some mix-up with that gym time. They got a last-minute gym booking for today so they're making this session optional, but – really – he should be there."

"How can they do that?"

I can hear the shrug in her voice. "They just do, Mavis. It happens. This is basketball."

"But, but ..." But when I said I'd drive Rory to basketball this year I didn't say I'd drop everything on a second's notice. I'm about to say it when I catch sight of my brother, stretching high, sinking a beautiful lay-up, landing with a massive grin on his face. "OK ... what are the details?"

"The gym's in Orleans, and the traffic will be terrible. You should have left five minutes ago."

"I just got home from the barn, and I smell, and ..."

"How do you think your brother will smell after an hour-and-a-half of basketball. Nobody will even notice you."

"Well, that makes it sound appealing ..."

But my mom's already talking, rattling off the directions to the gym in Orleans. "There are traffic circles there – you know how to get through them, right?" she asks.

I shove a water bottle under the faucet. What I feel like saying is, 'Have you ever heard of Gmaps? Because that's how I'll find this gym.' What I say is "Uh-huh."

I fill an extra water bottle and cram a bunch of banana-chocolate-chip muffins into a Ziploc bag for Rory and his buddy, while I pocket an apple for me. When I'm ready, I cut her off. "Mom, five minutes ago you said we should have left five minutes ago. I have to leave."

"OK," she says. "And, Mavis, about Ava's stuff ...?"

I wait for her to say she's sorry I had to get called out to Stonegate on such short notice. Instead she says, "Where do you plan to put all of it?"

Seriously? "I can tell you that now, or I can get Rory to basketball on time." *Sort of* on time.

I'm already clicking "end" on the call as she says, "OK, bye. We can talk about it later ..."

I stick my head out the door and yell, "The basketball bus leaves as soon as I tie my laces. Make sure you're ready!"

I find slip-on sneakers instead, shove my feet into them and bang the door shut behind me. "Come on, loser and ..." I lift one eyebrow in the direction of his new friend.

The guy grins and puts out a hand. "Lucas."

Lucas. My mind fills with a big chestnut face. With warm lips whiffling across my skin. So weird that I've never known another Lucas, and now I've met two in short succession. Even if one is a horse.

"Something wrong?" I've left him holding his sweat-and-ball-grime-encrusted hand out for longer than is really socially acceptable. The sweat on my hand's dried, but it's still seamed with horse grime. I shrug and accept his shake. "OK, Loser and Lucas – let's get you guys to basketball."

Chapter Nine

By the time I've sat through Rory and Lucas's try-out, battled my way back from the far east end of the city through a one-lane bottleneck caused by late-season construction, detoured to go to a drive-thru – without which Rory insisted he would faint – and dropped Lucas off at his house, I'm tired and there's no doubt about it – I do stink.

My mom was right; the guys smell too, but I was right that it doesn't make anything better.

I experience a tiny lift of relief when I pull into the driveway and the heap of Ava's stuff – shoved onto the as-phalt to make room for Rory and Lucas's basketball bags – is gone. I really didn't feel like carrying it inside.

"I want the shower," I tell Rory at the door.

He shrugs. "Whatever. I want dinner."

"I just took you to the drive-thru!"

"I just played ninety minutes of basketball."

I stop arguing at that point because I'm getting what I want – first dibs on the shower – if my mom's willing to let him scarf a second dinner that's her decision.

I don't want to see her just yet. Don't want discussions about what I've eaten, or if it's been enough. Don't feel like thanking her for dealing with Ava's equipment – even though I know I should.

Later. That can all wait for later.

Right now, I leave my shoes at the door and pad up the stairs planning to grab the t-shirt that's hanging on the back of my door, and my most comfortable pair of jersey shorts from the drawer, and head straight to the shower before anyone can beat me there.

I flick my bedroom light on and freeze.

The floor is covered with six horse blankets, and four sets of horse boots. There are saddles leaned against my bed. I can't even walk across my room to get to the drawer containing my shorts. In the middle of it all is a Sharpied note: *This is yours. Deal with it. Leaving it in the driveway is not acceptable.*

My first reaction is a strangled laugh. This is actually kind of funny. Even more so because I definitely didn't expect it from my straight-laced, serious, mother. When my dad said things were going to change around here, I thought of horses, and cars, and vacations, and clothing allowances. Maybe other things are changing, too ...

Good one, Mom. Even if I won't say it, I'm thinking it.

I forge a path through the clutter, grab my shorts, and head for the shower.

My mom might have made me laugh, but that doesn't mean I'm going to drop to my knees and clean my room immediately. Things can only change so much.

***

I dream of horses. How could I not? My room reeks. The more I thought about it, as I drifted off to sleep, the more amazed I was that my proper mother would allow all this stuff in her house. Doesn't she know even a stable as clean as the Stonegate barn is inevitably mouse-infested? And even when the pests aren't as big as mice, bugs galore have definitely burrowed in these items.

Still, the mess is here, and it's going nowhere, and the aroma from it means horses run through my mind as I sleep.

Not horses I've known. Not Pushkin, who I owned way back when riding was fun – the prettiest little palomino you could imagine with this crazy script-like scroll of words branded into her neck. Thinking back, it was probably cruel that somebody had done that to her, but it added to her charm. Everyone at the barn knew her and it made me proud to own a horse with those unique, exotic markings.

Not Ava, either, even though she and I campaigned so hard together. She slept in strange stalls while I slept in strange beds. We showed up at well-organized, and organized-chaos shows. We drank water that smelled and tasted funny to both of us. And our names were always read out together.

There are other horses I've known, too. Drew's mare, Serendipity, who I showed the season I was between horses. Others I climbed on when their owners were injured, or out of town – my long legs and starved physique, and red-ribbon reputation meaning I was a sought-after clutch rider to bring home a ribbon – to boost the value of a horse up for sale.

But the horse I think about has a badly home-permed forelock, and a rough coat. He's a chestnut – which has never been my favourite colour. The blaze on his face is dingy – more yellow than white. He's loud and demanding.

But he's loud and demanding for me. Or, at least, he was that once. He called me. He wanted me to stand by his side.

I don't think a horse has ever needed me, wanted me, chosen me. Turns out, now that one has, it's something I can't forget.

I wake up to Lucas tickling the back of my neck with his muzzle and realize, two seconds too late, it's actually a horsefly taking a chunk out of my unprotected skin.

That's it. These things have to get out of my room to-day.

I sit up in bed, hand clamped to the back of my neck, and wonder what on earth to do with a pile of horse gear in the middle of the city.

***

The answer to my what-am-I-going-to-do-with-all-the-horse-paraphernalia comes as I'm eating my granola. It's a text from Laney: **They like Ava. She vetted clean. Looking good for them to keep her.**

It's still early, and I'd be forgiven for my brain still being foggy, except the atmosphere in my room by the time I left this morning was also foggy – or something like it – so a lightbulb goes off pretty quickly. Good thing I found my phone, because this could solve all my problems: **I have a bunch of her gear – turnout blankets, saddle pads, boots – do you think they'd want it? It's all good quality.**

It's worth asking. If it's in good shape you could probably get a few hundred dollars for it.

I bite down on a satisfyingly crunchy nugget of granola. "If it's in good shape ..."

OK. I think I can handle that.

***

I'm in the laundromat – the one on the main street near my house, which I've never paid any attention to, except to notice the big, hand-lettered *No Horse Blankets* signs stuck in the window.

There are three machines whirring around containing Ava's blankets with some saddle pads, and various wraps thrown in for good measure.

I'm studying my timetable – it's handy having a keener for a brother – he went up to the school and brought both his and mine back with him.

I'm not worried about my courses, or even my teachers. I might not be able to get along with most people, but teachers are different. I generally show up for class – on time – get my work done – with good grades – and never text, or Snapchat, or update my Instagram account during class.

In other words, teachers like me.

What I'm more concerned about is the actual physical location of my classes within the school. I'm trying to figure out the optimum location for my locker; trying to minimize my daily steps.

Is it better to pick a locker near the door closest to our house, or one closest to my homeroom? But my homeroom will change in January ...

A girl sits down across the table from me, tapping long, black fingernails beside the hoof pick I found snagged in the strapping of one of the blankets. There's thick black liner around her eyes, and her lips are also black – although not as solidly so; her lipstick is wearing off in places – I can't stop staring at the flecks, as the face under all the kohl softens and she gushes, "I looove horses ... do you ride them?"

As long as I can remember, whenever anybody's asked me this, the answer has been, "Yes." Yes, I ride horses. Yes, they're sweet / cute / adorable. No, I'm not scared of them. Yes, I jump. These are the polite, meaningless answers you give when somebody – usually a woman; any shape or size from cotton-candy-pink-clad little girls, to grey-haired grandmas, asks about horses.

Lots of riders are proud – even a little smug – when they answer these questions. Over the last couple of years, I've become intensely bored by them. Now, I'm free, though. Now, I can say "No."

No. I let the word float in my head and wait for the happiness, the surge of giddiness, that's supposed to come with it.

This time, it doesn't come. The girl twirls my hoof pick around on the table top while a clench of anxiety tightens in me. Because if I don't ride horses, what do I do?

Nothing special.

The circling scrape of metal on Formica is driving me crazy. I slam my hand down on the pick. "Stop. Doing. That. Please."

I pull the hoof pick back toward me, and drop it into one of the two duffel bags I used to bring the blankets here.

Her face hardens again, to match the stark black she's adorned it with. "Wow. I guess you do ride horses. I guess you're one of those snobby, uptight horse girls everybody always writes books about." She deliberately turns, and stares at the **All-Weather Horseware** logo from one of Ava's blankets which has plastered itself against the washing machine glass and stays there for what feels like the longest ten seconds of my life.

The girl stands up, flicks the glass, and says, "There was no need to be so nasty. I just asked a question." Then she walks toward the counter.

Nasty. It would be nasty for her to tell the man behind the counter that I've got hairy, sweaty, muddy, *forbidden* horse blankets stuffed in three of their machines.

I'm pretty sure that's exactly what she's going to do.

I heave the duffel bags onto the table, pull the zippers all the way back, and yank the mouths open wide. Then I start pushing buttons on the washers.

I have no idea how they work. The doors are locked and I don't know if there's any way to disengage them before the cycle's completely over.

A glance over my shoulder shows the laundromat guy putting the phone down and leaning toward black-make-up girl.

I try every button, one after the other, then I start pressing multiple ones together. Finally, the first machine gives a long, shrill beep and stops whirring. While I wait for it to completely stop, I move onto the next machine, trying to replicate the sequence I used on the first one.

The blankets are still dripping but, fingers crossed, they're mostly clean. The last one is hanging out of the top of the duffel as I scoop both bags off the table and nearly collapse under their weight.

Ho-ly cow. Wet horse blankets are heavy.

The man is walking toward me, though, with wanna-be Goth-girl behind him. "Hey!" he's saying. "You wait a minute!"

"No! Sorry! Can't!" I'm leaving a long stream of drips behind me. "Just got an emergency phone call. Have to go!"

"This girl said you had horse blankets in those machines. No horse blankets allowed!" He points to the backward lettering of the sign, the sun shining around the stark letters. "There's a charge!"

I turn to hurl my back against the glass door and look him straight in the eye. "Her? That girl? She's cuckoo? Look at her – crazy – am I right? You can't listen to her."

I'm outside, which should make me happy, but the entire bottom half of both bags is soaked, and it feels like they're stuffed full of barbells.

There's a girl in front of me, staring. I guess the whole scene is just that bit too loud, and too weird – enough to make a passerby stop, anyway.

On closer inspection, I know this girl. Eleanor Parkes. We were in the same class for most of our Primary / Junior school careers. We were sort of friends back then - even though it was probably less her choice, and more our moms setting up play dates for us. She's tall and lean, but strong. I could use her muscles right now.

I gamble on her feeling some kind of rah-rah schooled-together loyalty. "Don't just stand there," I say. "Grab this bag."

She only hesitates for a second, before shrugging and taking the handle. "Where are we going?"

The laundromat door opens and Goth-girl's yelling, "I am not crazy, you bitch ..."

"Around the corner. Fast."

Lucky for me when I got here the only parking was at the end of a narrow alley running away from the laundromat. An alley with a second exit.

I yank the back door open, because it's faster than the car's super-slow-mo hatch, and say, "Here!" slinging my sopping duffel into the footwell, then standing back while Eleanor does the same.

The black nail-polished, lipsticked, eye-linered girl is halfway along the alley. "Thanks," I tell my once-upon-a-time friend. "I appreciate it." I nod toward the approaching threat. "I'd better go."

As I step into the car she asks, "What was that all about, anyway?"

"I'll tell you at school." I turn the ignition, fingers crossed that my locker will be nowhere near hers and I'll never have to explain.

"Bye!" I squeal the car out onto the wider street and peel away.

Chapter Ten

This time, when I pack the car full of Ava's things, it doesn't smell at all. There's no dirt left on them, and I'm guessing that spreading all the blankets around our backyard to dry in the breeze probably wicked away any lingering nasty odours.

Now everything just smells like sunshine and the outdoors.

It won't last long, but that's not my problem. I just need them to make a good first impression.

The parking area at Laney's is in front of the main barn. It's a large, low building, encompassing a long aisle of stalls, with a tack room, and feed room, an attached indoor arena, and even a lounge; small, but with heat and an indoor powder room.

When I first moved Ava here, coming from the relative luxury of Stonegate, it seemed small and clean enough, but definitely basic.

Compared to Lucas's small back barn, though, it's immensely fancy.

It's also not that cozy. I pile Ava's equipment on the lounge table, and realize it's probably natural for this barn not to feel homey to me. I no longer have any business here.

In Laney's last text she said she'd be going to Kingston on the weekend, and could take the stuff with her – all I needed to do was leave it in the lounge.

Which I've done.

So, I can leave now.

I step out of the barn and pause.

It's stupid, but I half expect Lucas to whinny for me again.

Which, of course, he won't. I might as well go.

The barn cat hurls herself against my leg, laying a thick carpet of tortoiseshell hairs across my shin, purring like a lawnmower.

Where I normally wouldn't bother with her, I'm happy for the excuse to linger. "Hey, you." I crouch down, to offer her a scratch, and in the way of cats the world over, now that I'm willing to give the attention, she doesn't want it. She stalks away, but soon pauses and looks back.

"Where are you going?" The answer is, toward the back barn. I guess I could take a few minutes to follow her ...

Our game of pet-purr-leave-follow continues until we're far past the main barn, and near the sand ring where Ava met her new owner. Meaning we're also very close to Lucas's barn.

I'm crouched, yet again, extending my hand to the cat and, suddenly, a rare feeling washes over me.

The words that come to mind are *quiet, peace, calm* ... things I don't feel often.

Maybe it's about the way this place is nestled in a clearing surrounded by tall trees. Maybe it's the air buzzing with cicadas, and singing with crickets. Or how the sun is so strong it feels like a hug, but without any of the normal summer sticky sweatiness.

Everything in me that's normally jumpy, or tense, or edgy, or on guard, is eased right now, and I don't want to mess with that.

The contrary cat, though, is happy to mess with my peace. She launches herself at me again; shoving her shoulders toward me.

Her purr bomb, coming just as I was lulled into tranquility, shocks me so I tumble backward and laugh out loud.

Immediately, a throaty whicker rumbles out through the barn window.

I must have imagined it. Or it was a big coincidence.

Only one way to know. "Lucas?"

As I rise to my feet the bedding rustles inside, then a big muzzle, edged with chestnut hair presses against the window bars.

No ...

"Seriously?"

By the time I cover the distance and make it into the barn there's a familiar bulky form, in a familiar colour, up by his stall door with his ears pricked forward.

"Wow," I say. "You work pretty hard at being cute, don't you?"

"Is he begging again?" Laney's in the doorway. She smiles. "He has a very effective technique. All big eyes and silent expectation. Here ..." she holds a carrot out to me.

I take it. "He wasn't so silent. He was whickering up a storm."

Laney's eyebrows lift. "Well that's out of character. He must like you or something."

I lay my hand on his stall door. "Is it OK ...?"

Laney nods. "Go ahead. Unlike the first time you met him, he normally does have good manners. I don't know what got into him that day."

I slide Lucas's door open and he pushes his white-blazed forehead toward me. I half-expect it to have a *Please scratch here* sign on it. What it does have are burrs.

"Again?" I use my free hand to pull one of them free. "Sorry," I explain to Laney. "I'm a bit OCD about manes and tails. I once actually dismounted in the warm-up ring to comb stray shavings out of Marcy Atkinson's horse's tail."

"You didn't!"

I nod. "I did. It was like my hands had a life of their own."

"Marcy must have been your main competition. You would have been better off to let her go into the ring like that."

"There's only so much I'll do to win." I immediately think of how much we paid for Ava precisely because she was red-ribbon-ready, and I wonder what it says about me that I'd let my dad pay for my wins, but I didn't want to beat Marcy by leaving shavings in her horse's tail.

Probably that I'm more than a *little* mane and tail obsessed.

Lucas has caught the scent of the carrot and, touchy as he is, I expect him to try to grab it from me the minute I hold it out. I'm ready to give him a stern warning about his manners, but he does this adorable bowing thing first, nose down, ears pitched forward. Something inside me unfolds. Something inside me breaks free.

"Hey bud ..." I offer the carrot and let him lip the top, then hold it tight. "Come on! Bite!"

There's a satisfying snap and the fresh, sweet smell of crushed carrot fills the air.

I turn back to Laney. "All Ava's gear is in the lounge. It's clean, so hopefully they want it."

Laney nods. "I'll take it with me this weekend. I don't see any reason why she wouldn't want it, but if not, it would mean you'd have to come back to pick up anything she doesn't take."

Her phone buzzes and she glances down. "I've been waiting for this text. I've got a load of shavings coming. They just turned off the highway – they'll be here in five minutes." She looks up. "Could you do me a favour?"

Please don't ask me to unload half-a-ton of shavings ... "Sure." My fingers are crossed. "Anything."

"I left Lucas in for the farrier to look him over, but he can go out now. Would you have time to turn him out?"

"Uh, sure. Yeah."

"Perfect! He goes out in the big field with the herd." She hands me his halter.

Block letters Sharpied on the inside of the nylon weave, catch my eye. They read, **Hazard**. "What's up with this?" I point to the word.

Laney looks at it and a little frown crosses her face. "Oh, yes. That's what his last owners called him." She shakes her head. "I have this belief in the power of names – that they have to be *right* ... Anyway, 'Hazard' just seemed too negative, and my mom's maiden name is 'Lucas,' and I wanted him to have a good start here, so I renamed him."

She fingers the fading "H." "You could take care of that – black out his old name and write in his new one ... although I guess you're done here ..."

Lucas noses into the halter I'm still holding and a tiny, achy pang hits me. If I'm done here, that means I'm done with him. He really is quite funny. And kind of cute – in a big, dusty, messy way.

Laney gives a little laugh. "It probably sounds silly to you, anyway – the name thing."

Em. For a second I imagine how it would feel if all my school notebooks and binders said *Em McElvoy*, if every time a teacher read out my name it was "Em," and no new person ever met me as "Mavis."

It would feel right in a way Mavis never has.

So, "No, I don't think it's silly," I say. "If I ever come out again, I'll bring a Sharpie."

***

At the gate Lucas stands and waits while I unclip his lead shank.

"Good boy," I say. "Off you go."

He doesn't budge.

I stroke his neck, then give one, firm pat, and say, "I don't have any treats. You might as well leave."

He just looks at me.

I walk behind him and give his rump a slap. "Go on you old silly. All the others are down there grazing. There won't be any grass left for you." As though to back me up a distant whinny floats up from the big field at the bottom of the hill.

He takes a sideways step, then hesitates. "Go!" I step away from him.

He steps, then I step, then he steps, and finally I'm through the gate and threading the chain through the bars. *Don't look up. Don't make eye contact.*

When I eventually do throw out a quick glance, he's moved about twenty feet, but he's stopped again and is looking back at me.

"Oh, for goodness sake! One of us has to go!"

That's you, I tell myself. *You are the human. You make the decisions. You leave.*

I don't trust myself to look back over my shoulder, though.

***

Laney's standing in the parking lot, watching the big truck trying to avoid low-hanging tree branches on one side, and a flower bed on the other, while it manoeuvres into position.

"Listen," she says. "About that thing we were talking about ..."

"What thing?"

"You having to drive all the way out here if there are any of Ava's things they don't want ... I was thinking ...

maybe I could make it worth your while." Almost before she's finished that sentence, though, she's shaking her head. "Actually, on second thought, forget it. It was a silly idea."

"What?" I don't know why curiosity always feels like a sign of weakness to me; possibly because, much as I try, I'm powerless to resist it.

"Nah, forget it. I mean, like I say, it probably won't happen anyway. She'll probably take everything and, if she doesn't, we can figure it out from there."

That curiosity again. It's there, but it's almost physically painful for me to show it. But it will be more painful to drive away not knowing what Laney was thinking about.

I try to sound as casual as I can. I even fake a yawn. "You might as well tell me. What's the worst that can happen?"

***

She wants me to ride Lucas.

That's all I really know, because right after she told me Lucas is some-kind-of-mix-that-definitely-includes-Quarter-Horse, and that she got him free when a local trail riding barn closed, and that she thinks she can turn him into an eventer, the driver turned off the engine of his rig, and climbed down. Laney said, "I've got to handle this, but you get the gist, right?"

I – too proud to admit that, truly, I have very little grasp on the gist, having never gone on a trail ride, or evented – nodded, and Laney grinned and said, "Perfect! We can talk more when I don't have a load of shavings waiting for me."

As I drive back to the highway, there's dust billowing in clouds around the car, bugs are splatting merrily on the windshield, the road is so rutted I think it might shake my wisdom teeth right out of my jawbone ... and I'm humming.

What?

I grip and flex my fingers on the steering wheel, take a long breath, search deep inside myself, and come up with a vague, tingly, floaty feeling I distantly recognize as happiness, founded on excitement. It's like those stabs of elation, of freedom, from when I first thought I'd quit riding, have taken root. It's less exhilarating, but more stable. Like it might still be here next time I go searching for it.

Considering Lucas is not my type of horse in any way imaginable, and considering I had given riding up and was delighted to have done so, I'm quite ridiculously, surprisingly looking forward to finding what happens when Laney tries to pawn Ava's old stuff off on her new owner and – oh yeah – to maybe have a ride on Lucas.

Chapter Eleven

I sit in the car and wait for my brother and strangely, unexpectedly, sitting here in my driveway is the most peaceful moment of my day.

The world continues by me – the kids who live at the end of the road wheeling by on their scooters, the older couple who walk their three terriers past our house at least twice a day – nobody notices me, sitting with the window open.

For a few minutes the September breeze luffs in the window, the still-warm-but-not-too-hot sun washes through the windshield, and I listen to birds singing, and a dog barking, and the little scootering kids laughing in the distance.

My gaze shifts to the rear-view mirror – to the bony knob of my wrist reflected and, possibly, magnified, in it. *Ugh.* My throat does this tightening, convulsing thing. *Yuck.*

I remember watching Grace get skinnier and skinnier all summer at the barn, but she never lost her natural athletic curviness. She was always pretty. That was obvious from watching Matt fall head-over-heels for her.

It used to make me jealous. Now I'm just resigned. I can be skinny, or I can be fat, but I'll never be pretty like Grace.

Maybe I should get a t-shirt that says, I starved myself for months and months, and all I got was this ugly, bony body.

My moment of peace and tranquility is definitely over.

I shift in my seat and swear under my breath, "Where the hell is he?" Then I lean on the horn and a cat, crossing our driveway, jumps and flees across the street, narrowly missing being run over by a delivery truck.

Rory pops open the hatchback and slings his basketball bag in. "Jeez," I say as he opens the passenger door. You nearly made me kill a cat ..."

"I did?"

"Yes, you did."

He shrugs. "OK, sorry. Is the cat dead?"

"No."

He puts on his widest smile, showing as many of his shiny white teeth as possible. "Well, that's good news, isn't it?"

"Shut up," I say, let out the clutch, and nearly roll over the same cat resuming her previous path.

I smack the steering wheel. "Come on!"

"Sorry," Rory says. "I'm pretty sure that was my fault, too."

"I hate you."

"I know."

***

"Don't forget to pick Lucas up," Rory says.

"I can't forget something nobody ever told me."

"Well, I'm telling you now – we need to pick Lucas up."

I sigh, indicate and merge into the right lane in preparation for the exit to Lucas's neighbourhood.

"Is this a thing? Us always picking Lucas up? And, if so, why?"

"Because his mom's just been hospitalized for depression and they only have one car, which his dad always has, either at work, or the hospital."

OK. That sucks. Lucas, like Rory, is always happy. And I'm a miserable bitch for moaning about giving him a lift to basketball.

"Yeah?" I gear down as we cruise along the ramp. "Well I asked for extra pickles at Subway today, and they only gave me the regular amount of pickles."

Rory nods. "That's practically the same thing."

"I'm glad you see that. My suffering is real."

"Excuse me while I just ..." He starts banging the right side of his body against the door, mimicking having a seizure. Or, at least, mimicking what he thinks it's like when he has a seizure. I get that he knows what it feels like, but I think I might actually know better than him what it looks like, since I've always been the one on the observing / calling for help end of things.

"BTP," I say. It means "Beyond the Pale." We reserve it for stuff that really, really bothers us.

It's more effective than any swear word, and it always get results.

He holds up his hands. "OK. Sorry. Couldn't resist."

"You should have."

I'm well aware it's harder for my brother to have his condition, than it is for me to live next to it. People like to remind me of that – I remember when I was younger and I told my mother I always worried a bit when I was home alone with Rory. She said "Well, think what it's like to actually be Rory and that might put your stress in perspective. You wouldn't trade places with him."

She was wrong, though. If someone told me, "You can take this on. This can be your burden, and your brother can get his driver's license, and go out on the basketball court and play as hard as he wants, and just generally go through life without thinking twice," – well, I think I would.

I guess that's easy to say when it's a hypothetical situation, but I'm aware of lots of ways I fall short in this world, and this one, I really mean.

I would give my brother my health if he wanted it.

I wouldn't give him my body, though.

I mean, who would want this rack of bones?

***

In the back of the car Rory and Lucas leap straight into a conversation they've had so many times before I know it off by heart.

"That science test ..." Rory starts.

"I know – did you see question seven? It was classic Mr. G – there were at least three correct answers but you can bet he'll only give credit for one."

"What did you put?"

"I said it was a solution."

"Yeah, see? That's right, but you could also say it was a mixture."

"I hate it when he does that ..."

I glance into the rear-view mirror. "Must be terrible to know you might only get thirty-four out of thirty-five. That one mark will probably keep you out of university."

Rory pauses just long enough to stick his tongue out, before turning back to Lucas, "It was like the mid-term last year. The multiple-choice section ...?"

It makes me wonder if this is why I don't have friends. Because I'm just not able to go over the same territory again, and again, and again. This type of small talk irritates me.

Thinking about my social shortcomings irritates me.

My irritation level continues to mount as I navigate our way to the gym.

Reason One: Traffic. "Why do they schedule your games downtown at the end of rush hour?" I ask. "Who does that?"

Reason Two: The empty seat beside me. Rory thinks it's polite, and considerate, and the right thing to do, to move to the backseat when Lucas gets in the car. "I don't want him to have to sit back there alone," he says. Stopped at a red light I catch the guy sitting idling next to us looking over at the empty seat next to me, then back at the two teenage guys chatting in the backseat. I stick my tongue out at the guy, then twist around under my seatbelt. "OK, that's it. I'm sick of feeling like a chauffeur. It's just weird that you two are sitting back there together."

Reason Three: The big, over-arching reason that's intensifying my annoyance with everything else around me. The Wall. As in Pink Floyd. My brother puts it on, then goes and sits in the backseat and engages in a lively discussion about chemistry tests and zone defense with his friend and I'm left listening to possibly the most depressing, dirge-like album ever created. I wonder if Lucas's mom was listening to it before she was hospitalized. Then I feel like a bitch for wondering that. *I. Cannot.*

Listen. To. This. For. One. More. Second. I almost say it, then I realize there's no need. I reach out, punch the audio button, and the noise disappears. Oh, sweet relief.

"Hey! Rory protests, but Lucas cuts him off with a laugh. "I was hoping you'd do that."

The light's changed so I keep my eyes forward but hold my hand up, palm turned backward towards Lucas. "High five, my friend. You can have a lift to basketball with us any day at all."

Chapter Twelve

It's the first Labour Day weekend I can remember that I've been here, at home, instead of showing at the provincial championships. While I'm glad not to be there, it also feels more than a little weird to be here.

I used to think, if I wasn't at a searing-hot-and-dusty – or freezing-cold-and-rainy – showground on this last long weekend before school, things would be so different. I'd show up on the first day with labeled and colour-coordinated notebooks. I'd have an honest-to-goodness "back to school" outfit, carefully selected, clean, and ready for Day One of classes. I'd, at the very least, not have cracked and broken fingernails with horse grime lurking under them.

All of which, apparently, is untrue. Because, the only notebooks I have are the ones still in my backpack from June, and everyone knows cute fall outfits are useless anyway, because it's still twenty-seven degrees and sunny at the beginning of September, and, as I head into the bathroom to brush my teeth, a text from Laney buzzes onto my phone: **By the way, if you want to work** with Lucas while I'm away this weekend, go ahead. I'll tell our neighbours who are taking care of the horses you might be by.

I stare at the screen. Hmm … do I want to work with Lucas this weekend?

On the one hand –*no*. This is my chance to take the first step toward at least pretending to be a normal social being – to go the mall which will be overrun with people from school. To maybe latch onto a group drinking bubble tea and gossiping about teachers. To at least try to launch my life of being a normal girl who doesn't drive to the country six times a week to ride horses.

On the other hand – *Lucas*. That whicker. And his big dark eyes. And the way he just stood and looked at me.

The voice. My mom's voice. She's on the phone, and she must be standing right by the vent in the kitchen.

I tiptoe to stand right next to it and crouch low just in time to hear her say, "… his flight gets in at noon … Yes, of course I'm excited – I already miss him more than I thought I would … no, it's fine – it's just that I've been so busy and want everything to be perfect when he gets here … Now that you mention it, that's a good point. There's no reason Mavis can't do that for me …"

I straighten. Whoa. "… *do that for me* …" It could be so many things. It could be clean the house from top to bottom. It could be mow the lawns and weed all the flower gardens. It could be doing all the time-consuming, fiddly prep – washing, and peeling, and chopping, and slicing, and dicing vegetables – for the fancy meal she's planned tonight to celebrate my dad being home.

Whatever it is, I don't want to do it.

Five minutes later I'm pulling out of the driveway with dirty hair, wearing dirty breeches, and with slightly fuzzy teeth.

As I slow at the first stop sign on my way out of the neighbourhood, my phone pings. Oh well – I'm not allowed to text while driving – my mom's made that clear many times.

I'll check it when I'm at the barn, safely, and if it's my mom maybe I'll even text her back and make a generous offer like buying some fancy bread or something on the way home.

Perfect. Yeah, that should do it.

The phone pings again, and I keep driving.

**

Lucas stands at the end of the lunge line, front legs splayed, head tilted, ears pointed at me and I know exactly what he's thinking. *You want me to do what?*

It's taken five minutes just to get him to stay out on the rail, while I walk back to the centre holding the line. Even now, it's clear one wrong move from me – and I'm not talking a big move; I'm talking a tiny, hardly perceptible, body language twitch which his horse radar will intercept in a flash – will prompt him to step forward and amble back to me.

Since I'm not that confident of my riding abilities when it comes to horses that somebody else hasn't already invested hundreds of hours of training into, and since the stable is just about deserted, I decided a simple lunging session would be the best place to start with Lucas.

What never occurred to me is that at least some of the hundreds of hours of training my horses have had, were probably hours on the lunge line. On the rare occasions I've been asked to lunge a horse, I just snapped on a line, picked up a whip, and off they went; circling around me, going up and down through their paces. I assumed horses were born knowing how to graze, swish flies, poop, and lunge.

Not so much. Not Lucas, anyway.

I take a deep breath. I know what I need to do. I need to get him to walk, but not *in*. *Forward*. I need him to walk in a circle around me.

I just don't know how to get him to do it.

It's a bit like learning to ride a bike. You've got to take a leap of faith and just go, so the momentum comes quickly, and you go straight and upright. If you're too slow, or uncertain, there are wobbles, and wobbles are fatal to bike riding, and to lunging.

I know that – in theory – I've seen enough people lunge horses, and lunge them well, to know what I should be trying to achieve. I just have very little practice achieving it myself. And considering I've owned two horses, that's not something to be proud of.

I throw my shoulders back, make a triangle with my lunge line and my lunge whip, and in my deepest, most authoritative voice, order, "Walk on!" Then I cluck. Then I wiggle the whip.

Lucas lifts a foreleg and I swear he's going to put it down facing me, and I swear if he does that I'll lose it, so I bellow again. "Walk! On!" and this time I give the whip a little swish, and he places his leg in front of him, away from the scary, swishy whip behind him, *on* the circle.

"Oh hallelujah!"

His ear swivels to me like he's thinking, 'Hallelujah sounds kind of like Lucas – do you want me to come in?' and I mutter "No, no, no," and I repeat. "Walk on!" and I've just been reminded losing my focus means losing his focus. *Concentrate ...*

I don't plan to lunge him long. You can't really, anyway. It's not great for horses to stay on a fairly tight circle for too long. It's not good for the people lunging them either. Even people who are good at it, tend to feel at least a little dizzy after a sustained session.

Given that Lucas has clearly never been lunged before – or certainly doesn't remember it – I expect he'll wear out quickly and I'll be able to take him in and hunt through his mane and tail to remove even the smallest snag of a burr and text Laney to say: I lunged him. No biggee. Job done. All uneventful.

Maybe not, though. Now that he's got the hang of it, Lucas is fine with lunging. After a couple of minutes of walking, it's easy to get him to trot.

He trots, and trots ... and his trot – well, let's just say it's not what I expected. That big hind end propels him forward and his whole body lifts. Lines of muscle pop out under his coat which, thanks to my vigorous pre-lunge grooming, already has a hint of something you might call sheen to it.

"Nice!"

It's the fox-faced girl. Where did she come from? Clearly, she's as sly as a fox, too.

"Hmm ..." I say.

"Don't you think his trot is nice? I would have thought he'd be all heavy and plodding – kind of shuffle around on the forehand – but he's beautiful, isn't he?"

"You're the expert." I've made sure not to meet her eyes even once.

A blur of motion tells me she's shaking her head. Vigorously. "No, not me – Laney's the expert. She said he could be an eventer – including doing dressage – and she wouldn't have said that if it wasn't true. And look at him ..."

There is a floatiness to him. Like he stays suspended for an extra half-second every time he takes a step. And where half a second isn't that long, all those fractions of a seconds add up to something beautiful as he keeps trotting.

And keeps trotting.

And keeps trotting.

I don't want to acknowledge this girl. Don't want to give her ideas that I like her, or need her.

But I also don't want to still be standing here with Lucas trotting around me an hour from now when I'm supposed to be halfway home for a family dinner.

I clear my throat. "There's just one problem."

"What's the problem?"

"He won't stop. He's been trotting and trotting, and I've been asking him to walk and he just keeps going."

"Oh ..." I look at her for the first time, and she tilts her head to the side. "Hmm ... Well, have you tried telling him to 'Whoa'?"

Lucas's ears flick to Fox Girl and he falters, then I say, "Whoa!" and he drops out of the trot like a stone.

Well, I'm an idiot.

I wait for the girl to gloat. To point out how stupid I am to have overlooked the complete slap-me-in-the-face obvious. To point out the one command that most trail horses are pretty much guaranteed to know, is "Whoa."

I let my resentment of her swell.

She grins. "Cool!" Then adds. "I'm super-glad we figured that out!"

"I ... uh, yeah. Me too."

A voice floats through the still air. "Sasha! Sa-sha!"

"Oh!" The girl jumps off the fence board she's been balancing on. "That's my mom. We're looking after the place while Laney's away. I'm supposed to be sweeping." She makes an eyes-crossed, nose-wrinkled face when she says "sweeping" and for a second I recognize her.

She is me.

She's already scampering away when I call, "Wait!"

She whips around. "Yes?"

"Thanks!"

She throws a thumbs-up my way and I make a mental note to sweep out the entire small barn when I put Lucas away. I guess I owe Fox Girl-Sasha at least that much.

Chapter Thirteen

"Your father's only home for one night. The team's first exhibition game is in just a couple of weeks. We're lucky he can get away at all, but he really wants to see you kids." My mom delivers the same facts to my brother and me, at the same time, but for two different reasons. To Rory, it's information. To me, it's a warning.

Her eyes rest on me for a second when she's done talking. *Be nice. Be kind. Behave.*

Even as my brother's nodding, my shoulders are tightening, neck tensing, jaw clenching.

My mom will never understand that she's better off not saying these kinds of things to me. She'll point to my prickly behaviour as the exact reason why she has to. I'll point back to her statements as the source of my ramped-up edginess.

And the fact is, we're both right.

I wonder what it's like to be sweet, and easy-going, and naturally friendly, like my brother.

Maybe I can do it. Just for one night. I can at least try.

It sounds good until we all sit down around the table.

My dad: So, are you kids excited about getting back to school on Tuesday?

Rory: Yeah, you know, my timetable's pretty good, and I'm going to try out for the school basketball team this year, and Mr. Simms is coaching, so that's cool, and maybe I can even sign up for Driver's Ed?

I cross my fingers under the table. *Please, please let Rory stay well enough to make the school basketball team. Please, please let him go another six months without a seizure so he can start learning to drive.*

My dad: Mavis?

Me: Huh? What?

My mom: School, Mavis.

Me: Oh, yeah. Sure. Fine.

My dad: How are you feeling about basketball Rory?

Rory: Lengthy answer involving excruciating (but endearing) detail on all the other players trying out, their relative strengths and weaknesses, what he would do if he was the coach, self-analysis on whether he's even deserving of making the team ... I tune out while I toy with a forkful of some kind of fancy rice dish and wish it was KD.

My dad: And you Mavis – Mom said you were riding today?

Me: No. I didn't ride.

My mom: Yes, you did Mavis. You texted me from the stables.

Me: I went to the barn. I didn't ride.

My dad: Well, we never expected Ava to sell so quickly – Mom said you did a great job writing up a posting for her – and we never expected you to quit riding entirely, so if you'd like us to pay for lessons ...

Me, interrupting: I'll let you know. It's all good for now.

Silence.

Rory: Hey Dad, I was checking out your team's website. I really like the logo. Do you think you could get me a cap, or a jersey or something?

My dad: Sure – it's probably not quite as cool as the merchandise from the big league.

Rory: Actually, I like it better. I'd for sure wear it.

My dad: Well, I'll definitely get you something ... and you, too, Mavis, if you want it.

Me *shrugging*: Sure. I guess. Fine. Thanks.

Silence.

My mom: This is delicious bread, Mavis.

Me: I got it half-price. It was day-old.

My mom looks like I've slapped her. My dad looks like he'd like to slap me. Rory just reaches for another slice of bread. "Well, if it was half-price you should have gotten twice as much. It's super-good."

Hands in the air. That's it. I will officially never be anywhere near as nice as my brother.

**

It gets better. It would have to. There need to be moments of something resembling family cohesion or my parents would kick me out of the house.

After dinner, in the ever-earlier dusk of the late-summer evening, Rory and I shoot hoops. It's so much cooler these days – as soon as the sun slips below the tops of the trees our breath puffs out into the crisp air – and that makes me happier. I'm not a sun-tan-beach-and-bikini type of girl. I prefer having my white skin covered. I like it when the mosquitos die off. The proper answer to my dad's question about going back to school would have been, "I'm fine with it. I like the weather. I do well in class." – that's what a polite version of me would have said.

My dad catches stray balls, and passes them back to us, and keeps score.

My mom comes onto the front porch, wiping her hands on a tea towel, and stands watching us, smiling.

When it gets so dark we can hardly see the net – when the second bat swoops low over our heads – we chuck the balls into the garage and roll the door closed.

Inside, in the hall, kicking our shoes off, Rory says, "Thanks Dad, that was fun."

He turns to me, "Nice shooting, Sis."

My dad smiles. "It was lots of fun. Thanks, Ror. Thanks Mavis."

Just like that, something clenches in me again.

At least this time I have the common sense to get out of Dodge before my prickles can show again. I point up the stairs. "I'm going to head up."

And I go.

Chapter Fourteen

It didn't take me long to figure out there's no point going home between the beginning and end of Rory's practices. I did it once and only had about half-an-hour before I had to turn around and leave again, during which time my mom called and asked me to peel potatoes and top-and-tail green beans so she could get dinner ready more quickly after she was done work.

So now I stay, and bring homework. Today I have a French grammar worksheet with me. I always intend to get all my work done. I mean, what better to do with my time when I'm stuck in a school – all the basketball gyms are always in schools – but there's this problem.

I really like basketball.

I find it impossible not to watch.

And tonight's practice is actually an exhibition game. Rory and Lucas's team is playing the elite-level team one age group down from theirs. They spent the last five minutes of the drive debating who would win.

Rory: "They're super good. They go to, like, eleven tournaments a year in Toronto. They even play in New York."

Lucas: "They're really small, though. We've got tonnes of height on them. There's no reason we shouldn't get every rebound."

Every point Rory made sounded legit, and everything Lucas countered with also made a lot of sense.

I want to see for myself. Age? Height? Skill? Or dumb luck? What's going to win this game?

***

Rory told me once, "You can cheer, but just don't yell my name. I hate that. It's so embarrassing."

I understood right away. When I was showing I was mostly too focused to truly hear what anyone other than the judge was saying, but there were moments when a voice would come through, and there was a big difference between hearing, "Good job," or "Nice work," and "Go, Mavis!"

It was usually my mother standing along the rails saying, "Go, Mavis!" or, worse, "Smile, Mavis!" or "Heels down, Mavis!" and then I'd think, *What do you think I'm trying to do, and what do you know about it, anyway?* And I'd wish she would just shut up.

One day, when she'd startled me, and I'd missed the judge's cue to canter, I'd blurted it out. "Oh, just *please* shut up!" and I'd immediately felt like one of those ridiculously spoiled little rich girls who happily spend their parents' money on horses, but then order them around all day – "Get me a lemonade, mother – and I mean a freshly-squeezed one, from the juice stand, not a can like you got me last time." Or, "If you want to be useful, you can buff the marks off my boots," – but instead of proving I wasn't one of them, by apologizing, I'd doubled down and refused to talk to my mom for the rest of the day.

It had worked; she'd mostly stopped coming to shows.

I like watching Rory play basketball too much to want to be banned from his games, so I stick to being the world's most inane fan, and yelling meaningless things, like, "Good hustle!" or "Go Stars!"

The exhibition game is really close – both Rory and Lucas were right – and the lead keeps swapping back and forth.

It's exciting, and exhausting. Which, I know, is pathetic because all I'm doing is rocking from one seat bone to another, clenching my fists, and clapping, while they're out there running, shoving, pushing, and sweating. Still, by half time I have a raging thirst and I hunt out a water fountain to fill up my empty water bottle.

When the bottle's halfway full – the little metre ticking over from proclaiming that this fountain has saved 1,927 plastic water bottles, to 1,928 – someone comes up and stands behind me, so close it's a definite invasion of personal space.

Do not look. Don't speed up. Take your time. Fill your bottle. In fact, I purposely break the stream at one point, just to make the personal-space-invader have to wait a little longer.

I slowly screw the lid back on, still standing in front of the fountain. When I turn around Lucas is standing there.

"Oh!" I say, "I thought you were somebody else!"

He puts his bottle under the stream and saves the world from its 1,929th plastic water bottle. "Who did you think I was?"

"A creep."

"Pardon me?"

"Just some random creepy person. Standing too close to me. But it's you."

"But if that random person was too close to you, then wasn't I too close, too? Does that make me creepy?"

"No." I sigh. Why doesn't he understand this? "It's you, and I know you, so the personal space boundaries are different. You stood acceptably close for how well I know you, but it would have been unacceptable for a complete stranger to stand that close."

"Really?" he asks. "How do you figure that?"

I shake my head. "Forget it. If you were a horse person, you'd understand. Horses are very aware of personal space. Just trust me – I'm right."

He takes a swig from his bottle then puts it back under the water stream to replace the water he just drank. "So, OK. I think I get it – maybe. But here's a question ... if I know you well enough to be within a more intimate personal space boundary than a complete stranger, then shouldn't I know your name by now?"

"I ... what? How do you not know my name?"

He shrugs. "Rory always calls you 'my sister' and we're at that weird point where I think everyone assumes I know your name, and it's become awkward to ask."

"But you just asked."

"I'm an awkward guy."

This is not – or at least, should not be – a difficult question. But I'm having trouble answering it.

Mavis. Lucas is right that Rory never calls me by my name. Maybe that's why he so rarely pisses me off. Because nothing gets my fists clenching and my teeth grinding like a sentence started with, "Mavis ..."

Laney's voice flashes through my head – her saying that names need to be right; that a new name can give you a new start – maybe I need a new start. Maybe this is the right time for it.

If I tell Lucas my name is Mavis, I'll always be Mavis, forever more.

"Em," I say. Maybe not confidently enough, because he lifts his eyebrows.

"M? Like the letter?"

I straighten my shoulders before I answer this time. "Em. Like 'E'-'M.' Em."

"Em," he says. "OK, that's easy. I guess that makes putting your name on a birthday cake pretty easy."

"Or monogramming handkerchiefs."

"Or addressing a valentine."

"Or ..."

It's a silly, funny conversation. It's not the kind of conversation someone named Mavis would have.

One of the other guys from the team walks by. "Thirty seconds," he warns.

Lucas caps his water bottle. "Well, it was nice to finally meet you properly, Em. And, I like your name. It's fun."

***

They win the game by a basket scored seven seconds before the buzzer. One of the moms sitting next to me leans over and pats my knee, "Oh wasn't that exciting?" Mavis would have pulled her knee away and maybe mumbled something like 'Sure,' or 'I guess.'

Em – *me*, oh wow; I just remembered "Em" is "me" backwards – laughs and says, "Very!"

I'm in the car, engine running, doors unlocked, as Lucas and Rory stride across the parking lot toward me. Rory opens the hatch and they both sling their bags inside. Rory gets in the backseat behind me, but Lucas drops into the front passenger seat.

"Hey!" Rory says. "What gives?"

"Em said she doesn't like feeling like a chauffeur. Since you didn't want to ride shotgun, I am. Plus, it means I can control the music."

"Em ..." Rory says.

I hold my breath. The wrong reaction from Rory could undo all the cool, happy, fun, confidence I got from going out on a limb and reverting to my way-back name.

"Yeah ..." he says. "I kind of forgot."

"For a smart guy, you sometimes have a terrible memory," Lucas says. "She didn't say it that long ago."

"You're right." Rory says. "I shouldn't have forgotten." His eye finds mine in the rear-view mirror and he winks.

Thanks, I think. *You're a good brother*, I think.

Now that I'm Em again, maybe I'll even find the guts to say it to him.

Another day. When Lucas isn't in the car.

***

Back at home, after we've dropped Lucas off, Rory unlocks the front door, then stops, barring my way.

"Hey!" I run into him. "Get out of my way."

"It's true I'd forgotten, but now I remember when that was your name," he says.

"Oh." Breath I didn't know I was holding whooshes out of me. "What do you remember?"

"It was before I was sick. Before you went to live with Aunt Mavis for that year. Dad used to be home more. You always had friends sleeping over." He shrugs. "Those things are what I remember."

"Better times," I say.

He shrugs again. "*Other* times. These times can still be good."

Oh, my optimistic, sunny brother.

"Thanks for the drive, Em," he says, and despite myself, I smile.

Chapter Fifteen

"**W**hoa!"

Thank God that works. Otherwise – well – otherwise, I don't know what. Lucas would be doing gallop circuits of the ring. Or, if he can jump the way Laney seems to think he can jump, he'd have jumped both of us out and we'd be off across the fields.

Why did I say I'd do this, again?

Everything I thought about this sweet-natured, stocky, gentle horse is wrong.

The lunge line taught me he can trot forever.

Getting on his back confirms Ava was even easier to ride than I ever imagined.

When I swung up from the mounting block, into the saddle Laney provided – seconded from one of her ancient, bombproof school horses – I expected to settle into something like a comfy armchair. I thought my legs would be spread so wide I'll be walking bow-legged for the next few days. I got ready to kick, and cluck, and I held my crop at the ready.

But Lucas is thinner than I imagined. Sure, he's deep-chested, and sure he's got a nice wide ribcage, but his actual heartgirth – where my legs lie – is relatively narrow. I recently had what might be my last growth spurt and my new, longer, legs wrap nicely around him.

Once on his back – in a supremely unnecessary move – I used all my aids at once. Taking no contact on the reins, I clucked, squeezed, and wriggled my butt.

Lucas shot forward, away from the mounting block, in a weaving trajectory. I imagined him saying, 'I'm going! I'm going! But you didn't tell me where!'

Which is when I first used the "Whoa" Fox-Girl suggested for lunging.

Sure, it works, but the idea was to ride this horse. Not to stand stock still in the ring.

I try moving one more time, lighter on the aids this time, but Lucas's sensitivity metre is on hair-trigger and he lurches ahead again, like a big drunken guy on a small rickety bike.

I grab the reins which, instead of slowing him down, makes his strides come shorter, but quicker so we're doing a mincing, jogging, sideways jig. The contact doesn't do much to steer him either. It's like when I was first learning to drive and I did what my dad called "cowboy lane changes" on the highway – "You don't yank the steering wheel from side-to-side," he'd said, fists clenched on the dashboard. "Steering is subtle. Gradual."

After that he'd paid for me to take after-school Driver's Ed lessons.

I ride Lucas for ten minutes and it goes like this. I squeeze. He walks. Then he walks faster. I tighten the reins. He walks faster. I tighten the reins again. He jogs. I can't decide whether to accept his unasked-for trot and rise to it, or whether to sit. If I sit, I bounce, and he trots faster. If I rise, he leaps forward, and – yup – trots faster.

I try steering him in tiny circles, but he's amazingly flexible and he seems to use the centrifugal force he gathers in them to come out going even faster.

I hate every minute of this. I'm rigid, tense, clenched. I want to cry.

The only thing that works is yelling, "Whoa!" and that just makes him stop dead. Which feels safer than bombing around the ring, but is definitely not productive.

We've gone through this cycle a few times, and he's haring down the long side in what must be a beautiful extended trot if you're not on his back terrified and not knowing how to control it, when fatigue washes over me and I decide if he's still running through the corner, I'll use my magic "Whoa" again, and I'll give up.

In that moment of capitulation, I must also relax for about two seconds – long enough to loosen the reins – and he slows.

He doesn't stop dead, but his forward momentum eases.

I'm scared out of my mind to do it, but I give him another inch of reins. He transitions from extended to working trot.

Oh. That's better. I can rise to this. I do, and everything is smoother, and he slows again.

No. Way.

I jam my heels down and push my hands forward and he – *Oh. My. God.* – he reaches for the bit.

It feels so good I just concentrate on not changing anything for a half-circuit of the ring, but I'm tired, and I'm afraid my luck can only last so long, so I slow my posting, and remind myself not to tighten the reins, and sit up straighter and ask him to "Walk" – not "Whoa" – and he does. He even maintains contact during the transition.

I can't believe it.

"Wow! Great! Give him a long rein!"

I let the reins out, and Lucas snatches all of them and stretches his head long and low, and Laney, checking-in from a lesson she's teaching in the other ring, says. "He looked beautiful, Mavis."

And I think, I need to tell her my name's actually Em, and I need her never to know about the disastrous twenty minutes that proceeded the blissful three-minutes she witnessed.

***

"I saw him running away with you." I spin around to see skinny-Sasha-fox standing in the doorway to Lucas's small barn.

"Excuse me?" I step out from behind Lucas where I'm extricating a burr from his tail that somehow escaped my earlier grooming.

She shifts from foot to foot. "I got here early for my lesson and I went to the upper sand ring for a minute."

"You don't know what you saw."

"I saw him trotting the fastest I've ever seen a horse trot and you couldn't rise fast enough to keep up to him."

I bite the inside of my lip. "Did you say you got here early?" I take an exaggerated look at my watch. "Because it's not early now, and unless you already have your horse tacked up you're going to be late, and Laney hates it when people are late for her lessons ..."

I say my last words into empty air. Sasha's gone, and she's taken her sharp eyes, and tongue, and too-big-for-her-britches attitude with her.

There. That's better.

***

When I pull into the driveway at home, there's a text on my phone.

Laney: They bought all Ava's stuff. I have cash for you. You left before I could hand it over.

Me: You were teaching. I didn't think I should interrupt. I can come out another time.

Laney: If you can make it early Saturday I can give you and Lucas a bit of time before my regular group lessons start.

Oh. Hmm. Those last five minutes on Lucas were fun.

But I'm supposed to be done with riding.

But they were fun.

But ...

Me: Let me check a couple of things and get back to you.

Laney: OK. Hope you can make it!

This thing happens – like a strange internal flutter; just like when Lucas nickers for me, or when he bowed his head for the carrot I gave him – it must be the feeling of resistance crumbling, because instead of walking up the path to the front door, I'm sitting in the car, texting: Actually, it looks fine. I can be there. See you then.

***

I'm at home, flossing, when I notice the achiness in my jaw, and teeth. Something was bugging me all through dinner, but I couldn't pin it down.

Now, though, as I pay attention to each tooth, I realize my whole mouth is sore.

Weird. I wonder why.

I floss the next tooth, then stare at the mirror, poking at my jaw. I can't find a specific source for the pain, but it's definitely there.

I take my hands away, close my mouth, then close it harder. Yup, there it is – *ouch* – as my jaw muscles tense the ache intensifies.

I have a flashback to me, jostling, jouncing, bouncing all over Lucas's back. Just remembering my whole body stiffens to resist the motion.

Including my jaw.

Bingo.

I start flossing again. Slowly, carefully.

If I had a human that tense on my back, I might run away from her, too.

Chapter Sixteen

Friday night. No moon. Rain pouring out of heavy clouds. Narrow undivided highway running between yet-unharvested corn fields.

The only thing that would be worse than the way the headlights glare, and shine, and splinter light around the asphalt would be having no headlights at all ... but it wouldn't be much worse.

A hulking pick-up flies by in the opposite direction so close I have to re-double my white-knuckled grip on the steering wheel of my tiny car against its buffeting.

Suddenly the interior dome light goes on and now I really can't see anything. "Rory!" I yell. "What are you doing?"

"My stats. I need to get caught up."

My dad thinks it's a sign of athletic commitment that my brother keeps a binder of his team's stats each year. My mom thinks it signifies mathematical genius. I generally consider it yet stronger proof of his quirky geekiness.

Tonight, I think it might get us killed.

"Rory! You cannot do that now. I can't see anything!"

"Just a second. I need to get this one last thing down ..."

"Rory ...!"

"Turn off the light!" Lucas's voice is deep, strong, and it rings with authority.

It shocks us both out of our bickering, and Rory turns off the light.

Into the newly dark silence, a deer leaps out of the corn about fifty feet in front of the car.

Oh. My. God. Ohmygod-ohmygod-ohmygod ... Now I see how people die when they hit deer. Now I see how the most solid part of her body would hit exactly at windshield height.

Breathe and brake. The words float into my head as one of the things my dad said to me before he handed my driving education over to the pros. *Breathe and brake.*

I do. The breath I take reminds me to brake as smoothly as I can, eyes open, hands on the wheel, not panicking.

And, as it turns out, we're farther from the deer than I thought, or she's faster, because she takes a couple of quick, scrabbling steps, then flings herself into the corn on the other side of the highway, and it's as though she was never there.

Except for the hammering of my heart, and the giddy lightness in my head.

"Whoa ..." I flex my fingers open, then shut again. Breathe again. "Thanks," I say. And it's a thanks to Lucas for getting Rory to turn that light off, and to my dad for giving me great advice, and to the cosmos for deciding Rory, and Lucas, and I didn't need to be a newspaper headline: Three teens killed in car crash on way to basketball game.

"You're welcome," Rory says.

My breath quickens, and my blood pumps, and if I wasn't driving I'd leap into the back seat and grab his throat. "Don't you even ...!"

"You did great. That was good driving. We're fine." This time Lucas's words are much quieter, but just as effective.

I calm. "OK."

While I'm glancing at him, a path of light spills between the front seats, and I look in the rear-view mirror to see Rory, head down over his stats sheet, wearing a headlamp.

I shake my head and Lucas says, "I know; you're thinking if he had that all along, why did he turn on the overhead light?"

"No. What I'm actually thinking is, what kind of teenage guy carries a headlamp around in his basketball bag so he can do stats in the dark?"

Lucas lets out what I can only describe as a guffaw, and it's a combination of his laughter and my relief, that sets me laughing, too, and we finally cruise off the dark highway into the parking lot of the rural high school we're aiming for, with my stomach hurting and Rory, in the backseat, asking, "What? What's so funny?"

***

It's a game that neither team can be particularly proud of.

Which happens, sometimes. I've had a couple of shows like that – where Ava and I won a ribbon, not because we were great, but because we weren't as badly off our game as everybody else. Victory by default – that's what it looks like Rory's team is cruising to.

There's frustration in the air, on the court, and in the bleachers.

It's hard to watch, but I'm sure it's much harder to play. I imagine myself on Ava on one of those under-performing days – think of what I'd have wanted to hear from the sidelines – and stay quiet. Sometimes silence is golden.

I wish everybody thought so.

There's this one guy – there's always one guy, isn't there? – one of the parents from our team told me he used to be an assistant coach for the other team until he got too many technical fouls and was fired from the coaching staff. Which is quite a feat considering all the coaches are volunteers to start with.

He's been grumbling, and rumbling, and muttering since the game started. As it's moved on, he's added in the occasional yell – "Ref!" or "Come *on*!" or "What was that?"

Next, he starts in on the players. Mostly keeping his comments too quick, or too indistinct for anyone to really catch properly. And then Rory gives the guy the exact opening he's been waiting for. It's true that my brother makes a complete mess-up of a pass, but it's also true it's the kind of mess-up that can happen to anyone, and especially to a frustrated teenager playing in a sloppy game.

"That kid might be big, but he's kinda dumb," the big, dumb former-assistant coach says, and everything in me promptly spikes. Adrenaline, blood pressure, heart rate, and breathing – all through the roof together.

At the last second, I remember *breathe and brake*. It's worked for me once already today, so I breathe, get control, then lean forward and tap the guy on the shoulder.

He turns around, all jowls and flushed cheeks, and I point at Rory and say, "That's my brother." Then I point at another parent. "And that's the mother of the kid you said was slow. And, guess what? The kids you've called fat, and lazy – their families are here too. And you know what we're all thinking?" I drop my eyes to his beer gut and stare openly. "We're thinking you'd have fun trying to keep up with any of them, and we're also thinking the dumbest person in this gym is the one slagging off other people's kids right in front of them."

OK, so I might have let the brakes out a bit, there. Hot on the heels of my adrenaline rush, fear hits me and I think – *Crap! What if he hits me?* – but he doesn't.

He says, "Whoa, what's your problem, girl?" and he leaves the bench, and I sit with my heart thudding, and my hands shaking, wondering if I might just be the one with the problem, and whether everyone around me now thinks I'm the big-mouth.

There's a tap on my shoulder and I prepare to turn and be told off, and a guy leans over and hands me a cold can of Diet Coke. "I've seen you drinking this. I thought you might like it. Thanks."

The woman sitting next to him nods. "Yes. Thank you," and a man on my other side says, "It was about time somebody said something to him. I just wish it had been me."

Oh. OK. I did alright.

Just as I'm relaxing, Rory squares up and swishes a three-pointer through the basket. I think, *That's going in* ... with just enough time to raise my phone and get a shot – not of the actual basket – but of Rory jumping in celebration.

With my dad's *breathe and brake* advice fresh in my mind, I find his number, attach the photo and text **That's a big three from Rory.**

Then I settle down to watch their team pull it together and win with at least some semblance of style.

***

Rory's pestering the dad who kept score for a copy of the stats. Normally I'd be riding him to get a move on but, realistically, I don't have anywhere else to be, and besides I'm feeling very kindly disposed toward my brother right now. He pulled up his socks. He played well.

Also, I'm enjoying staring at the back of Lucas's head as he changes his shoes. Because he's so much taller than me I've never noticed it before, but with him sitting down I can see he has a double crown with the hair whorling in two distinct spirals.

It's kind of cute.

I can't believe I'm thinking that.

He turns to find my eyes on him, and before I can blush, he says, "My sources tell me something happened during the game."

"Huh?"

"In the stands. I hear there was nearly a fistfight."

I stand up straighter. "Oh yeah? What exactly do your sources say happened?"

"I heard that bonehead dude who used to be a coach slagged off the wrong player, and said player's sister told him where to go."

"Hmm …" I say. "Did your source tell you what the bonehead said about you?"

"What?"

"He said you were funny-looking."

"And what did you say?"

I shrug. "What could I say? It's not slander if it's true."

"Ouch," he says. "I feel like I need to go into the change room and comb my hair."

"Except I bet you don't have a comb."

He grins. "Busted."

"Whatever. I wouldn't worry about it. I've already seen you like this. It's too late to change my first impression, anyway."

Chapter Seventeen

I'm already in the kitchen when my mom yawns her way in. She slept on her right side – it's not just the flat matting of her hair that gives it away, it's also the shadow of yesterday's make-up smudging her right cheek.

She blinks twice when she sees me. "And what, may I ask, has you up and making toast this early on a Saturday morning?"

I stick my knife into the peanut butter. "Rory has basketball today. And I have to take him."

"Rory has basketball at noon. Rory won't get out of bed until 11:00."

"Yeah, well Rory doesn't have a horse to ride before basketball. By the time I get out there, and ride, and get back, and have a shower ..."

"Hmm ... a shower, huh? Who are you, and what have you done with my daughter, because she would definitely drive her brother to basketball covered in horse manure ... does this have something to do with the fact that you're driving Lucas as well?"

I snort. "Absolutely. Driving two of them means the car will stink doubly of basketball sweat. At least one person has to be clean."

My mom snaps her fingers. "Speaking of which, can you remind your brother to put his shoes in the basement? He left them in the front hall last night and the fumes nearly overcame me when I got in from work."

I shake my head. "Not my responsibility – I'm just the driver."

There's this weird fizzing excitement in me. Finishing my last ride on Lucas on a five-minute high seems to be carrying over to make me look forward to this morning's ride.

Maybe we can pick up where we left off. Maybe I can accomplish something else in my riding. Maybe Lucas and I can actually learn something together.

The anticipation has me in a good enough mood, that when my mom shuffles off to the shower, I measure out the coffee and turn the coffee maker on, and the last thing I see as I pull out of the driveway is her in the doorway pointing to the steaming mug in her hand and blowing me a kiss.

It's surprisingly easy – and nice – to make my mother's day.

***

In fact, there's such a warm fuzzy glow in my middle from making coffee for my mom, that I stop at the last Timmie's before the barn and pick up two hot drinks; hot chocolate for me, and coffee for Laney. I don't know how Laney takes her coffee – don't know if she even drinks coffee – but I figure it's hard to go wrong with a double-double and, for $1.59, it's worth taking a chance.

Although riders can be the earliest of early birds when it's for a horse show, today is not a show day, and the only vehicles in the parking lot when I pull in belong to the barn and the barn staff.

The morning air is cool enough to make the heat of the cups in my hands very welcome. I hold them in front of me and, as soon as they clear the threshold of the small barn, Lucas does his usual spin-rush-hustle-whicker.

"Hey buddy," I say.

There's a second rustle from the stall across the way and I turn to see Laney lifting a pitchfork of manure into the wheelbarrow. "You've got a fan." She nods in Lucas's direction.

"Yeah," I say. "I think he has an affection disorder or something."

"He doesn't do it for me."

"He doesn't?" A warm glow spreads through my gut. Really? I'm special? Or at least Lucas thinks I'm special?

"Do you bribe him with Timmies?" Now she's nodding toward the cups in my hands.

"Oh, no. This bribe is for you. If you like coffee, that is." I hold out the cup containing the coffee.

Laney grins. "You'll never catch me saying no to coffee." She leans her fork against the side of the stall and takes a swallow. "Mmm ... so good ... thanks for this Mavis – it was very kind of you."

Funny, Mavis already sounds like somebody else's name.

When I don't answer right away, Laney continues. "I think you'll find a certain someone in this barn came in with a tail full of burrs. If you want to clear those out while I finish this stall, I have an idea for something we can try. If you're up for it, that is."

***

The thing we try is fun, but hard work.

Essentially Laney shuts Lucas and me in a sand ring and says "Go! Have fun!"

At first, I don't know what to do, but she says, "Come on, Mavis – how often do you get a whole sand ring to yourself? Run!"

She says it like it's some kind of treat; being invited to run in deep, sucking sandy footing. It's so, so difficult and by the time I've gone to one end and back again, there's already sweat pricking along my hairline – despite the morning still being quite cool – and my lungs are burning, and chest heaving.

I keep going because Lucas doesn't give me much choice. He follows me.

It's the most unexpected, endearing, completely over-the-top-adorable, thing I've ever seen.

He has really cute ears and they pitch forward, and he trots after me. If he was a dog, I swear his tail would be wagging.

There are jumps set up in the ring and when I dart around them, he chases me.

"Jump one of them!" Laney calls, and even though the last thing I need is more exertion, I pick a low X and hop over it, and Lucas follows me.

When I'm so tired I can't pick up my feet anymore, I stop. Lucas wanders up to me.

"Go ahead," I tell him. "You're free." I wink at Laney. "How often do you get a whole sand ring to yourself?"

But he won't go. He just sniffs me all over, then lifts his muzzle to my shoulder and rests it there.

"Stubborn ..." I mutter. But I lift my hand and scratch at his cheekbone and, kind of like the Grinch, I swear my heart grows – if not three sizes, at least one-and-a-half.

Laney opens the gate wide. "Good job! Come on out."

She holds out the lead shank and I take it from her and clip it to Lucas's halter, even though I'm sure he'd just walk beside me all the way back to the barn. Still, loose horses are never a good idea. A barking dog could run at him. Another horse could distract him. There are lots of reasons why it's safer to have him on a lead ... but it's nice to know I probably don't *need* it to keep him with me.

"When I saw how much he wants to bond with you, I thought doing this would be really worthwhile," Laney says. "Of course, if you still want to have a ride, we can tack him up."

"Oh no, that's fine." I shrug, like I don't care, but a) I'm completely worn out, and b) based on our first ride, I can't guarantee ending on such a positive note again if I get on his back this morning.

"Isn't he sweet?" Laney asks.

"He's got quite a personality."

"Do you see why I didn't want to call him Hazard? There's no way it fits."

I take a deep breath, square my shoulders, and decide this is as good a time as any to have this awkward conversation with Laney, "About that – about names that fit, or don't – even though Mavis is my full given name and it's what everybody's called me for a long time, I've never felt like it *fit*."

"Oh?"

My cheeks are hot. Laney is so perfectly together from her clothes, to her voice, to the way she acts around people and horses, to her name, which just seems like it was made for her. She must think I'm weird, crazy, eccentric, flaky, or even worse.

"Yeah. So, I've been wanting to go back to what I used to be called – a long time ago – even though some people might think it's not a proper name but, well, I feel like it suits me better and, anyway, yeah. That's it."

Laney tilts her head. "So, what is this weird first name?"

Great. In my big, brave speech I still haven't told her my name. Now the burning is spreading from my cheeks down my neck. "It's ... um ... Em."

She smiles. "Em, huh? Well, I don't know what's not proper about that, and I think you look much more like an Em, than a Mavis."

It's only when I exhale that I realize I've been holding my breath. "Really?"

She nods. "Oh yeah, and you're talking to an 'Elaine' – not that there's anything wrong with that name, but I never felt like it suited me."

"Elaine! My grade two teacher was named Mme. Elaine and not only did she speak French with a horrible accent, but she used to make me go sit in the corner for fidgeting at my desk. I *hated* her." I gulp. *Whoops.* Maybe too vehement. I rush to add, "You're right, though – not that there's anything wrong with the name."

Laney laughs. "Well she sounds like a mean teacher, so I'm glad you don't have to associate me with her. For me Laney just works better."

"Cool," I say.

"Cool, Em," she says.

I like Laney.

The name and the person.

***

I've turned Lucas out with his tail braided and bagged, as an optimistic defense against all the burrs I've been combing out. I'm thinking the most likely scenario is that he'll leave the tail bag in the burr bush, when Laney falls in step beside me.

"So," she says.

"So." I say.

"I need to ask your opinion of Lucas."

"In what way?"

"I got a call from this guy. He owns Silver Spurs farm – you know it?"

I nod. It's a kind of all-purpose, strawberry-picking, pumpkin-patch, hayride place on one of the major roads into the city.

"Well, he's thinking now that the trail-riding place Lucas came from shut down, he might start offering rides at his place. He figures it would be a good addition to what he already does."

"I can see that, I guess." But I can't figure out why Laney's changed the subject.

"He heard I have Lucas – he knows he's an experienced trail horse. He's interested in buying him."

"What?!? But you said Lucas could be an eventer. You were giving him a fresh start."

"Yes," she says. "That was the idea, but realistically, I don't have the time to work with him right now. You're the only one who's lunged him or ridden him. Which is why I'm running this by you. Logically, selling him to a place where he'll be well-treated, and he'll be doing something he already knows how to do makes sense. Especially when I have no time to turn him into this eventer that lives only in my imagination."

But, but, but, but ... "But ..."

"But, what?" Laney asks. "I'm willing to be – no, I'm *wanting* to be – convinced to keep him, so if you've got something for me ..."

What am I supposed to say? That he'll definitely be a super-successful eventer, and he'll always be sound, and she'll regret it forever if she sells him now? I don't have anywhere near the expertise to say that.

It hits me like a basketball in the solar plexus – I'll miss him. That's why Laney should keep him. Because I'll miss him if she doesn't. Which I doubt is a compelling argument.

"I think ..." I say.

"You think, what?"

Oh, just say it. "I think I'll miss him if you sell him."

She stops walking, and the sound of my boots alone crunching on the gravel brings me to a stop as well. "Well, you could take him on."

"I ... what?"

"You've gotten to know him a bit already. Do you think you could make him your official project – until I have time to ride him – and then he wouldn't be sitting around being wasted?"

But ...

But, I collect red ribbons in the hunter ring. That's what I do.

But, this was never the plan.

But, I've never trained a horse. I'm not good enough. I don't know what I'm doing – there are lots of ways of saying it, but the bottom line is, I'll probably fail.

"What do you think?" Laney prompts.

"I think I have to think about it."

"Fair enough." She starts walking again. "Just, if you could, don't think too long."

"Yeah. I hear you."

***

I turn out of the driveway and all I can think about is coming back and Lucas not being here.

I think I'd stop coming.

I pull over, struggle my phone out of my back pocket and text Laney. I'll do it.

Press send, then add. What if it goes wrong?

I'm waiting, indicator on, to accelerate onto the highway when her text comes back.

Steer to the shoulder. Find phone. Read text.

It won't. I'll help.

Chapter Eighteen

I'm staring at my stirrup. It's not that high, but it's completely out of my reach after all that running-through-deep-sand stuff Laney had me doing on the weekend.

I know because I've lifted my foot toward it, twice, and twice I've had to stand back down on the mounting block.

Yes, the mounting block. That's how pathetically sore I am. I'm already standing several feet off the ground, and I still can't manoeuvre my foot into the stirrup.

"Hey, what's up?" Laney says as she strolls into the ring.

Not me. Obviously.

"Um, I'm having a little trouble here."

Little furrows appear between Laney's eyebrows. "What kind of trouble?"

"I, uh, I can't get up. I mean, I can't lift my foot ... I mean I'm really stiff ..." This is a great start to my brave new adventure with Lucas ...

"Oh!" Laney's face clears. "You overdid it? No probs. You just do this." She reaches over and with a quick flick of her wrists, slides the stirrup down about six holes. "There, try that. We'll just re-adjust it when you're up."

How dumb am I? How could I not have figured that out for myself? If Laney somehow didn't know already, now she'll definitely see how woefully unsuited I am to take responsibility for training a green horse.

Even though the stirrup is now almost even with my foot – even though all I have to do is lift my foot a couple of inches and slide it forward – it still kills. But I'm not about to look whiny, on top of clueless, by complaining to Laney about it.

I slide my foot in, and swing over Lucas's back, and let's just say it's a good thing I have momentum, and it happens quickly, so I move right through the worst of the agony and land in the saddle with the pain just a burning memory in my muscles.

"Ouch?" Laney asks.

"You could say that."

"What were you doing that made you so stiff?"

I stare at her. Does she really not remember? "Um, all that running around I did with him last time?"

She tilts her head to the side. "Really? That's it?"

I'm starting to get the feeling it's the wrong answer, but I can't see any way of backing out now. "It was hard work. The footing's deeper than it looks."

She kicks at the footing in question. "I'll give you that it's not running on smooth pavement, but it wasn't *that* much work."

I open my mouth, "I ..." then shut it again. What can I say? 'Yes, it was?' What's the point in arguing? Laney just had to let my stirrup down like she would for a nearly incapacitated rider – obviously she knows it was hard for me.

She wrinkles her brow. "In all that showing you've been doing for the last few years, weren't you training?"

I stare at her. "Um, yeah, like every day."

Her brow furrows deeper. "Like cross-training? Running, or cycling, or weights, or yoga?"

I'm honestly perplexed. "I *rode*." Laney, of all people, should know what a work-out riding is. I shouldn't have to convince her how wrong the old "horse-does-all-the-work" myth is.

She shakes her head. "Not good enough. Start with three runs a week. A total mileage of ten kilometres. Then we'll work up from there."

It doesn't sound like she's asking. It sounds like she's ordering. For a brand new agreement that came together from a chat in the driveway, this is starting to sound pretty serious. Why does she even care how fit I am?

The way her arms are crossed, though, and the tempo of her tapping foot, keep me from asking.

Shut up and ride. I reach down to shorten my stirrup so I can do just that.

* * *

It's like before.

Me: Tense, grip, squeeze, cluck – the only thing I don't do is wriggle because my muscles are too tight to do that.

Lucas: Leap, skitter, trot – extremely fast – nearly bump me out of the saddle.

Me: Oh crap. *Bounce.* Seize reins. *Lurch.*

Lucas: The devil is on my back and I'm going to run away from her!

Me: Oh yeah. Forgot. Damn. "Whoa!"

Lucas: Halt. Immediately.

Me: Sides heaving with a wicked combination of terror and exertion made worse by the fact that some movement involved in the little jumps Laney got me to do really tugged on my core, so every muscle involved with breathing in any way is sending up a major protest with each deep inhale. *Ouch. Oh. Hurts.*

Laney, who's been watching our double-panic-attack act from the centre of the ring finally speaks up. "So. That didn't work, did it?"

This is a new kind of coaching. I'm used to people watching Ava trot around with me on her back saying, "Looks good enough, Mavis. Remember your hand position, Mavis. Heels down, Mavis."

Laney is direct, and forceful, and has high expectations.

I can't answer her. If I answer I'll cry. I can't do this. I'm terrible. I'm awful. I'm going to ruin this horse. I should just back out right now. Tell her to sell Lucas. Go back to my short-lived plan of being a mall-haunting, Netflix-watching, non-horseback rider.

"Em!" Laney's voice is edged with whipcrack. "I asked you a question! Answer me. Did. That. Work?"

"No," I gasp. Shake my head. "No."

"Alright," Laney says. "Give him a scratch on the withers, tell him everything's OK, and let's start fresh."

Something in those words tugs at me. *Start fresh.*

They sound hopeful. They sound promising. They sound – for a brief second, anyway – possible.

I like the idea of getting a second chance. Of trying again. Of clearing away the bad and aiming for the good.

"Em?" Laney asks, and a little bit because she's making the effort to use my new name, but mostly because she's not going anywhere and I don't really have a choice, I say, "I'll try."

I struggle to remember last time I rode Lucas – that one sweet moment – how did it happen? What did I do?

Not much. Barely anything at all.

Which is probably just as well considering my abused-by-overuse leg muscles are not enjoying being wrapped around a horse and I'm not sure there's much they can do right now.

I breathe, and think *Walk*, in a kind of whispering thought, and just as I go to grab my reins, I remember *Don't!*

Lucas's first step is a lurch. Coiled energy jumping forward. But then he finds nothing to pull against and he slows, and one ear flicks back like he's asking "Are you still there?"

"OK," Laney says. "Now help him. Don't pull, but just take up enough rein to give him some support."

I try to be subtle, to be gradual, but he still tenses and quickens his steps.

"That's fine," Laney says. "Ignore that little burst. Leave your contact like that until he gets used to it. It won't take long."

Another ear flick and, she's right, he backs off again.

"Why does he do that? I mean, I thought trail horses were dead slow plodders. I thought I'd have to wear spurs and use a crop to get him to move at all. But he's a total runaway."

Laney's walking beside us now. "Take up one more notch of contact ... wait, hold it ... good. Leave it there for a few steps." She squints up at me. "So, imagine this. All your life you've walked in a long line of horses – the same horses – with your nose up another horse's bum. You've never had to make decisions for yourself. And, you've probably never been ridden by the same person twice and every rider who's been on your back has either not given you any support at all, or has reefed the heck out of your mouth at every opportunity, and maybe done some kicking and yelling to go along with it."

"Oh-kay ..."

"Another notch in the reins, Em."

"Better?" I ask.

"About halfway to having normal contact." She flips back to talking about Lucas. "So, what do you think happens when you're a young, strong, fit horse and you get taken away from your friends, and your routine, and the only kind of riding you've ever known?"

You're scared. You run. You're difficult.

I want to lean over and give Lucas a great big hug and say "You're OK" and "Nobody will hurt you" and "You'll be fine."

That's not what he needs, though. I know what he needs. At least I think I know what he needs in this moment.

I roll my shoulders back to disperse any lingering tension, and I will my hands to be *light, light, light,* and I take up one more careful notch on the reins, so Lucas can actually feel me and I can feel him and this time he doesn't even accelerate when I do it. He just gives a grinding chew on the bit.

"Exactly," Laney says. "He already likes you, but he needs to learn to trust you. And I hope you're patient because trust is a long-term thing."

***

I've never had a lesson like it before. And by "like it" I mean a lesson where I don't leave the walk. At least not intentionally – Lucas's panicked scooting at the beginning of the lesson doesn't count.

When we finally, finally get Lucas to walk calmly forward on a light, but existent contact, Laney tells me to halt him and start all over again.

I don't want to. I just got him walking sanely. This is going to ruin everything.

Laney raises one eyebrow and I'm scared. There's a wall in her – a hard core – that I've never seen before. Today I've learned she'll yell at me if I don't do what she asks.

I bring Lucas to a halt.

It's forty-five minutes of halt ... walk quickly ... calm down slightly ... walk sensibly ... and halt again.

Getting that first reasonable walk took the better part of ten minutes. By the end we go around the ring in a halt-walk, halt-walk pattern. Consistent, calm, and, on the very last one Lucas puts an arch in his neck, drops his head perpendicular with the ground, mouths the bit gently, and holds it through both the up and down transitions.

"A-a-a-nd *that* is where we quit!" Laney says. "Give him a long rein and a good scratch on the withers."

Lucas drops his nose to the ground and there's a new, loose swing to his strides which is when I realize the tightness is gone from my muscles, too.

For now. I guess it could come back, but after wincing my way down every staircase at school – and our school has a *lot* of staircases – and deciding it was too far to walk home for lunch – which tells you something because the cafeteria special today was Mexican Meatloaf – it's very nice to have legs that feel normal again.

Laney claps her hands together. "That was so great! I feel so good about our progress!"

I guide Lucas into the middle of the sand ring. "Um ... we didn't leave the walk."

She laughs. "Um ... yeah, but we did everything *properly*, so when we do leave the walk it will be brilliant." She reaches out and gives Lucas a scratch on his neck. "So, any questions about today?"

I hesitate. I'm not used to lessons being a two-way thing. Throughout my riding life, my coaches have told me to do stuff, I've done it more or less resentfully, more or less successfully (often less successfully) and that was it. Same time, same place, next week. But Laney did ask ...

"You've never taught me like that before."

She tilts her head and squints against a slanting shaft of the lowering sun. "You've never ridden like that."

Which, OK, yeah, is actually a fair point.

What I just did wasn't the kind of perch-in-an-expensive-saddle-and-tick-all-the-equitation-boxes kind of riding that's been earning me red ribbons on Ava for the last couple of years.

It was focused on small details, and tiny adjustments. It involved my brain as much as my body. To anyone watching it would probably be pretty boring.

It was cool. I liked it.

"Go on," Laney gives Lucas's rump a light slap. "Take him in. There's a shaving you missed in his tail."

"What!?!" I twist around in the worn saddle and strain to peer over his solid backside.

"Ha! Just kidding." Laney winks. "Or am I?"

That's it. I've got to get this horse into the barn and check out his tail. I can almost feel that one, solitary, jagged shaving mocking my grooming efforts.

I throw up my hands. "I give up! I don't want to be a rider. I just want to be a groom."

Laney says, "Well, that would be a shame, because I'm thinking, if you keep working this way, you could end up being a pretty darn good rider."

It's a funny compliment for me to be happy about. Last year, at this time, I was in final preparations to ship off to the last of the big Ontario fall shows, and trying to decide where we should stable in Florida for the approaching January classic. Before I sold Ava, I had so many ribbons I started giving them away to the grandmother of one of the girls I showed with; she used them to make quilts.

Most people would think I was already a pretty good rider. Most people would wonder what the heck Laney's talking about.

Not Laney, and not me. We both know the truth.

I was afraid of her finding out, but I realize she knew from the beginning – that genie was never in the bottle. The miracle is that she gave me this chance at all and I have to fight down the part of me that's tempted to ask why. That is definitely a question for another day ... if ever. Right now, I'm happy she thinks I "could end up being a pretty darn good rider."

Chapter Nineteen

I regularly drop in to the pharmacy, or the supermarket, or wherever I need to go on my way home from riding. It only makes sense to get my errands done when I'm already on the way home.

And, yeah, when I do my hair is always helmet-flat and, sure, there's generally a slash of something which, if DNA tested would contain various horse bodily fluids, across my shirt, and, OK, I often smell.

I never feel self-conscious, though. Ever. Unlike right now, where I'm in the privacy of my front hall, wearing what most people would probably consider quite normal clothes – shorts, a t-shirt, and running shoes – and I feel like a complete and total dork. As though stepping out of that front door will be the hardest thing I've done in a long time. Because right after doing that, I'll have to start running, and *that* is something I am totally unfamiliar with, and unprepared for.

I'm positive the sight of me, attempting any kind of run cadence on public streets, will lead to people pointing, and whispering, and asking, 'What does she think she's doing?'

But Laney told me to do it. Laney said ten kilometres in a week. So, if I don't get my butt in gear and run three-point-three-three-three kilometres today, well, I'm in danger of having to run five kilometres twice later on, or – God forbid – ten kilometres in one single day.

Also, I have to drive Rory and Lucas to practice later, and I want to make sure I have time for a shower first. And, yeah, my mom's right that if I was just driving my brother, a shower wouldn't be a priority. But I'm not just driving him. I'm driving Lucas. And Lucas has been known to stand really close to me, and I've been known to like it, so ... a post-run shower is a must.

Which means, I'd better go.

I learn a few things.

1) Starting fast is a bad idea.

2) Walking is not necessarily the nice break it should be – it's much, much harder to get going again after.

3) A steady pace is my friend.

4) Three-point-three-three-three kilometres is surprisingly far.

It takes me nearly half-an-hour – which is quite a bit longer than my overly optimistic target. Which means that shower is going to be more like quick rinse.

As soon as I get home, before I even take my running shoes off, I stick my head inside the door and yell, "Hey,

Ror! I'm having a two-minute shower and we're going –
be ready!"

Shoes off, in the house, door closed. No sign of my
brother. "Ror!?!"

I carry my shoes inside to put them by the side basement door where my mom likes smelly shoes parked, and
yell one more time. "Rory McElvoy!"

He appears from the kitchen holding a bowl overflow-
ing with Cheerios – a spoon sticking rakishly out the side.
"Geez, sis. Keep your shirt on!" He's wearing the stretchy
shorts he sleeps in and an ancient, hole-dotted t-shirt
showing Fido-Dido holding a can of 7UP.

"Rory, how are you not ready for basketball? I nearly
killed myself running to get here on time and you're in
your PJs?"

He glances into the kitchen toward the microwave
display. "Actually, doesn't look like you're exactly on
time."

"I ..." I throw up my hands. "That's my point. I've been
moving as fast as I can so we're not late and look at you."

He shoves a spoonful of Cheerios in his mouth and
grins around them. "Canceled."

"Maybe if you were less disgusting, and able to sepa-
rate the acts of eating and speaking, I would know what
you just said."

He swallows. "Practice. Is. Canceled. Tonight. There – is that clear enough?" He waves his spoon in the air. "Some band night, or play, or something at the high school. They're using the gym."

"Seriously? Seriously! I love how people tell me things around here."

Rory shrugs. "Whatever. At least now you've got time to work on that big Bio lab I heard everyone moaning about today."

At which point I whip one of my running shoes at Rory's head.

He sidesteps, my shoe leaves a smudgy mark on the door trim, and Rory laughs. "Another bonus of not having to go back out – you'll have time to clean up your mess before Mom gets home."

I give him the finger and slam my way back out the front door.

It's a gorgeous night. There won't be that many more warm nights with late-evening flaring sunsets. And, sure, I should probably be glad not to be sitting in a stinky gym.

But ... but I just hate it when plans change and nobody tells me. That's what's bugging me so much.

It's got nothing to do with the warm fuzzy feeling I've had all day at the thought of Lucas sitting next to me in the passenger seat. Lucas protecting me from Rory's musical taste. Lucas joining seamlessly into the banter between my brother and me, except sometimes – kind of sweetly – taking my side.

I'm just mad I hurried when I didn't need to.

That's it.

I toe my feet into the flip-flops I left by the door earlier today and head to the car. When I got home from school I didn't even take my bag into the house – just put it straight in the car to take with me. Now because of the stupid last-minute change in plans, I need to bring the stupid bag inside.

There's a basketball in the way that I hopped over on my run into the house. I pick it up now on the grounds I'm likely to forget about it and break my ankle tripping over it on my way back. "... bloody Rory ... can't put his own stuff away ..."

I've always loved the nubby surface of a basketball. This one is sun-warmed and has a satisfying feel – at the same time solid and hollow. I smack it with the palm of my hand and it sends up a ringing internal echo.

I dribble – once, twice: *smack, smack* – and it comes back to me in a rush. Five years ago – or six – when Rory was coming off his first season of house league. When his brain had just started to wrap around the amount of strategy involved in the game – I knew, because he used to try to talk to me about it for hours on end. He grew twelve centimetres that year, and people were starting to look at him twice when he walked into a gym.

"I want to go competitive next season," he'd told his coach, and his coach had said, "Well, then. Fifty free throws a day. Do it all summer and we'll see how you look in the fall."

Rory shot not just fifty, but at least a hundred free throws every day, along with practicing lay-ups and basic dribbling. It was his get-out-of-day-camp-free ticket.

I, less lucky, was enrolled in a series of increasingly boring camps. Week Three of the summer saw me start a "Girls in the Kitchen" camp. The first day I arrived home an hour before camp let out.

"What are you doing here?" my mother wanted to know.

"I guess that's a good question for the camp managers ..." I'd said.

My mom and I came to an agreement; I could stay home from camp if I never – like not ever, once – bugged her. It helped that the camp refunded the registration fees when she asked them how a twelve-year-old was able to wander off unnoticed halfway through the afternoon.

And I started counting free throws for my brother. Sitting in the shade with a school notebook I'd brought home full of unused pages and a sharpened pencil, I kept his stats. Attempts, baskets – those broken down into "rim" "swish" and "lucky bounce" – and whatever else we thought would be fun on any particular day. Backward shots. Shots taken from behind the fire hydrant.

Shots taken by his sister.

I got good that summer. By the end of August, I had a nearly seventy per cent average.

Now, holding the ball, I know exactly how to weight it in my fingertips. I remember how my knees should bend. I instinctively follow through – reaching for the rim even as the ball's already out of my hands – flying for the basket.

It's a swish. A total and complete beautiful swish.

OK. I have to try that again.

I quickly remember another thing about shooting free throws. Man, is it addictive ...

When I make one, I think, *Hmm ...* I'm pretty sure I can do that again.

When I miss, I think, *One more try ...* I'll sink the next one.

I count by tens. Six out of ten. Yuck.

Then eight out of ten. Not bad.

I wonder, wonder, wonder, if I try really super hard, and concentrate my entire mind on it, whether I can get ten.

One – swish ... Two – backboard ... Three – swish ... Four – very, *very* lucky bounce ... Five and six – swish,

swish ... Seven and eight ... both drop in off the backboard ... Nine – more good luck ...

And now – holy crap; no pressure except that I've just sunk nine in a row and there's one more basket between me and a perfect ten – yikes.

I dribble, dribble. Exhale. Dribble again. Bend my knees and think *Just let it go, Em.* Just release and follow through. Just do it.

It goes. It hits the rim. It circles, and circles, and circles and it starts to tip out – I clench my fists – and it makes one more half circle and topples inward, through the basket.

"Yessss!" I jump and laugh, and someone else is yelling, "Yes!" too.

I whirl around, and Lucas is in the shade by the hedge dividing our lawn from our neighbours', on his bike, one foot resting on the curb.

I reach for the ball before it bounces onto the street and say, "How long have you been there?"

"Well, let's just say, from what I've seen it looks like you have a hundred per cent free throw rate."

My cheeks are hot, and me thinking about how hot they are makes them even warmer.

I shrug. "It's just that easy. I'm not sure why you guys have so much trouble hitting yours."

He drops his bike to the lawn. "OK. Free throw challenge. Best out of ten. If we're tied, best out of five. After that, sudden death."

"For what?"

"What do you mean, for what?"

"I mean what are the stakes? Since, apparently, you guys don't have practice tonight, there are way more important things I could be doing with my time."

I don't even know how I want him to answer. I'd be disappointed if he said "five bucks," but I'd be terrified if he said, "dinner and a movie."

He reaches for the ball, but I don't let go of it. "Hmm ... stakes ... lemme think ..."

He gives the ball a tug and because I'm off-guard, gets it. Takes one quick glance at the basket, lines up his shot and lets it fly.

Swish!

"Beat that!" he says.

Because I've won in the show ring so easily, for so long, with so little invested in the effort, I've forgotten what it's like to have competition race my pulse. Forgotten the pressure of wanting to rise to a challenge.

"Oh!" I grab the loose ball and think *knees, hands, breathe,* and swish my own shot. "There!"

It's only when we're tied at nine out of ten, and we're both a bit short of breath and I, for one, am sweaty in my long breeches that I remember about the bet.

"OK," Lucas says. "Best out of five now."

He reaches for the ball I'm holding and I swing it out of his way. "Nuh-uh. Not until you tell me what we're playing for. Otherwise I'm going inside to change."

I'm braced for him to lunge for the ball, but he doesn't. Instead he stands very still and looks me straight in the eye and a slow smile spreads across his face, and I've felt this way before – I've felt it when I'm about to open my sealed report card, and I know I got straight As, or when the horse show announcer is calling out the winning numbers in reverse order and I know she's going to end with mine in first, or on Christmas when the box in front of me is exactly the right shape and size to hold the new riding boots I circled in the saddlery catalogue – something I want is about to happen.

"Yo! I'm here!" Rory steps out the door, still in a reasonable facsimile of his pyjamas, but now with shoes on, and a second basketball under his arm.

Both Lucas and I swing to face him, and he bounce passes his ball to Lucas. "What's with the face, Sis? You don't look that glad to see me. Afraid I'm going to beat you?"

"I'd be careful what you say," Lucas says. "Her stats would knock you over."

Whatever was there with Lucas – whatever promise, or possibility, or tension, or whatever it was – is gone. "Shoot, Em! Show him what you can do," Lucas says, and he's friendly, and grinning, and funny, and nothing else.

Maybe I imagined it.

I don't have time to dwell on it, because Rory shoots his ball right after mine – trying to knock it out of the basket – which leads to a three-player, two-ball scramble full of grabbing, stealing, and a fair bit of body-checking.

It's so much fun, I don't even notice I'm having fun – if that makes any sense. All I'm thinking about is making sure I come up with one of the two balls as often as possible, and that I miss the worst of the guys' body slams, because unlike the last time I played pick-up with my brother, now he really is much bigger, and much stronger than me and it has nothing to do with how often he works out, and how infrequently I do. Rory and Lucas combined have a good foot in height on me, and no matter where I fall on the skinny-versus-chubby version of myself, they also probably outweigh me by at least sixty pounds.

It means I have to be fast, nimble, and sneaky. It means I run a lot. It means I probably didn't need to put in my three-point-three-three kilometre run earlier on – this is probably doing it.

I've just grabbed the ball from between Rory's legs and pulled up for a nice swish from not-quite-but-nearly three-point range, when the second interruption of the night comes.

"Hi Lucas." The "hi" is long and drawn out, like "hi-ee-ee ..." and I whip around to face Eleanor, the girl I haven't seen since she helped save my butt outside the laundromat.

My heart sinks because that single, simple word – that "Hi" – is intimate, and sweet, and teasing, and easy, in a way I could never make any word sound, and it's coming from a girl with long, long, white-blond hair that usually waves down her back but tonight is thick in a foot-long fish-tail braid. She wears micro-short shorts that would get a curvy girl sent home for dress-code violations, but her thighs are impossibly long – just bone clothed in a light coating of muscle and milky-white skin – which keeps her just the pretty / athletic side of outright sexy. From the classes I've had with her, I know her average sits steady between eighty and ninety, she appears in at least one of the school's drama shows each year, and she runs cross-country in the fall, track in the spring. I'm pretty sure she's going to be elected to a position on student council.

In other words, she's perfect, and clearly Lucas has noticed her long before today, because his, "Oh, hey Ellie," is also warm and happy, and accompanied by a smile I've suddenly realized I want just for me.

Before I can decide I hate her for every petty, uncharitable reason under the sun, she flicks her eyes at my brother, and the smooth skin on her cheeks flames a deep pink, and she looks down at the driveway and half-whispers, "Hi Rory."

Rory hasn't paused. While Lucas and I have been distracted he's been racking up the points. He shoots the ball, and throws a, "Yeah, hi," over his shoulder before lunging to try to get his own rebound before Lucas does.

At which point she turns to me and says, "You owe me!"

"Pardon?"

"An explanation?" she says. "The exact last words you said to me were 'I'll tell you at school,' before you left me in an alley with some foaming-at-the-mouth Goth girl charging toward me." She throws her hands up. "I had to run for my life."

I dribble the ball once. "Good thing you run cross-country."

She laughs, like I made a joke. "Seriously, I've been trying to catch up with you in Bio every day, but I have the worst seat ever ..." She shakes her head. "My mom made a dentist's appointment for me on the first day of school – who does that? Anyway, when I finally got there on the second day, I was stuck sitting way in the back corner and you're up at the front, and you always bolt and I can never catch you, so ..." She actually pauses to breathe. "... what was that all about?"

"Trust me," I say. "It was way more boring than it looked."

"Oh, come on," she says. "You can't just leave me hanging like that."

I'm being honest, though. It *is* boring – really. I mean, now that they're sold, I have no interest in Ava's old winter blankets. I can't imagine this girl, with her full life, wanting to hear the story about how I got them clean enough to sell. It would be like Rory and Lucas, having their endless, circling, meaningless conversations.

"But ... but ..." she says.

"Hey, I didn't know you two were friends." Lucas has stepped away from the net for a few seconds to come talk to us.

We're not. Honest-to-God my mouth is open to say it. People like Eleanor can have their pick of friends, and they don't go around picking people like me.

"We are!" Her arm slides through mine and when she bounces on her toes it travels through me. "We've had some big adventures together!"

"Cool," Lucas says. He looks at me. "Ellie lives three doors down from me. But, then again, maybe you already know that ..."

Rory bounces a ball off Lucas's back then, two seconds later, the other one bounces off the back of his head. "Come on!" he yells. "We have, like, a few minutes left until it's pitch black. Let's play some more."

Lucas shakes his head. "Nah, like you say, it's getting dark. I should probably walk Ellie home."

It's kind of far. I'm glad I'm not walking that far. *Wait ... oh ...*

"It's kind of far," I say. "Do you guys want a ride home?"

"Really?" Ellie asks. "You wouldn't mind?"

Lucas answers. "Of course she wouldn't – you guys are friends."

Yeah. That's it. Of course. We're friends.

Rory comes in the car, too, and on the way home, while we wait for a traffic light to turn green, I say, "That girl likes you. God knows why."

"Funny," he says. "I was just about to say the exact same thing."

Chapter Twenty

In the morning, I shuffle-bump down the stairs on my bum.

The tightness in my quads will literally not allow me to make the motion necessary to walk downstairs.

I eat my cereal then return to the bottom of the stairs and stare up, wishing I'd had the foresight to shower and get dressed before I came down for breakfast.

I have no idea how I'm going to get around at school today. For that matter, I have no idea how I'm going to get to school.

One thing at a time. I have to get upstairs first.

Rory comes up behind me. "What's up?" he asks. "Contemplating the state of the world?"

"Buzz off."

He shrugs. "Fine. Whatever. Sorry for asking."

"No. Wait."

He pauses. "Yes?"

"I can't walk."

He laughs. "Um, yes you can. Since you were about nine months old, according to Mom, which is when you started cruising toward ungated stairs, open water, and anything else that could give her a heart attack."

"Thanks for reminding me I'm a perpetual source of aggravation in this family but, seriously, I ran yesterday, then we shot all those hoops, and now my legs are just, kind of, seized up."

"Seized up?"

I nod. "Like when you were in grade nine and the grade twelve class designed a weight program for your class as part of their end-of-year project, and they made you do so much in one class you couldn't even lift up your fork to eat dinner. Except with me, it's my legs."

"Walk up sideways," he says.

"Huh?"

"Try it."

I feel stupid doing it, but when I turn sideways and lift my leg to the first step, it's slightly better. Not perfect, but better.

"It's going to take me forever to get upstairs like this," I say.

"But are you going to get there?" Rory asks. Without waiting for my answer, he bows and says, "You can thank me later. And when you're up there, take an ibuprofen. And make your shower nice and steamy – it'll loosen your muscles. And come down the stairs backwards."

***

As the day progresses, my muscle pain diminishes. Probably partly on its own, and partly because I live dangerously and pop another ibuprofen before the six-hour window has ended from the first one I took.

Biology is my last class of the day. We sit at elevated lab tables designed for two students and it's the second class in a row I've sat alone. It seems like my former Bio partner has dropped the course.

It's probably the subject matter. It's probably not me. At least that's what I'm telling myself.

I'm not alone for long.

Ellie eases onto the tall stool next to me, then hooks her long, strong, non-seized-up legs around the bars.

"Hi," she says. "Thanks for the lift last night. I had to get up for cross-country practice at seven-fifteen this morning and I would have been wiped if I had to walk home."

Meantime I'm staring at small things I've never noticed before. Like the patches she has sewn on her back pack that say I'm Burning up a Sun just to Say Good-Bye and I'm the New Doctor. Like her t-shirt that says I Found This Humerus with a picture of a bone next to it.

Ellie is a geek in pretty-girl clothing. No wonder she likes my brother.

"What?" she asks, and I'm saved from admitting I've been reading her bag, and her clothes, by the teacher calling out the attendance. We both answer our names and she turns to me. "Wow – it always sounds so funny to me when they call you Mavis in attendance. I mean, you are so much an Em."

"I guess he didn't get the memo ... wait ... since when do you think I'm an Em?'"

"Since forever," she says. "Since that time – remember – when I had my tenth birthday party on the same day as Alanna Hardy's and she told everybody I picked it on purpose to be mean to her, and all the other girls went to her party, and you were the only one who came to mine, and we got to eat all the junk food my mom got for, like, eight girls." She takes one of the post-long-sentence breaths I'm getting used to. "It was nice of you."

I could use this as evidence for Laney's name theory – see? I was a better person when I was called Em – but, in reality, I probably wasn't invited to Alanna Hardy's party, and my mom would have made me go to Ellie's anyway.

It's so weird that I don't remember it at all – it's like mean-girl Mavis erased all my other memories – but Ellie clearly does remember, so I mumble, "Yeah, right. Junk food."

She's already onto the next topic, though. "I thought ..." she glances to the back of the class where the girl she normally sits with is giggling with the guy at the next lab table, "... I thought we could maybe pair up for the next lab? I feel like we have similar work ethics."

What she means is she normally gets nineties, and so do I. The girl at the back, who is now leaning so far toward the next table that she's in danger of falling off her stool, is solidly in the low-seventies range.

"OK," I say.

"Yeah?"

"Yeah. Deal."

She holds out her hand and I realize she wants us to shake on it – further evidence of geekiness.

Whatever. If it makes her happy. I have to turn slightly to reach my hand out to hers, and it twinges a shot of pain through my still-tender legs.

"You OK?" she asks.

"Fine."

She looks at me, eyebrows raised, waiting, until the extreme awkwardness of it makes me say, "My legs hurt a bit. I overdid my exercise last night."

"Oh! I know some great stretches. Just come to the back field with me after class and I'll show you."

I'm going to say *no, that's fine, forget it.* Then I look at her perfectly shaped, lovely legs and shrug. "OK, I guess. I have a few minutes."

"Perfect. We'll fix you right up."

Chapter
Twenty-One

Wow. Ellie's stretches were the bomb. Once I stopped looking over my shoulder – once she said, "Nobody is looking – believe me," and I gave up my grip on embarrassment and imitated her as best as my stiff body could, I felt much, much better.

Not perfect, but well enough to be rumbling along the dirt road on my way to the barn actively looking forward to getting there.

It's a new feeling for me. Before now going to the barn was always something I ticked off my to-do list. Ava had to be ridden six times a week. *Six-five-four-three-two-one ...* check. Done for the week. Start again next week.

If I try to remember a time when riding wasn't a job – not a countdown or a chore – it was when I won a lot less, showed a lot less; even rode a lot less. Even though I remember a happy hazy time involving a bunch of little girls and our ponies, realistically I was probably only at the barn every other day, at the most. The better I did, the more I rode, and the more I rode the less I liked it. Near the end, with Ava, I'm afraid I was very close to hating it.

Which is why this sense of peace, relief, and calm, that washes over me as I near the turn-off to Laney's place is so noticeably different.

***

It's nice to hear Lucas greeting me with his deep vibrating nicker.

I've become slightly obsessed with hearing it, and I shamelessly call out to him when I'm still several paces from the barn. "Hey buddy! I'm here. Say hi!"

He always does, today included, except today there's something extra. Today his whicker is followed immediately by his face. Then his body. Strolling out the barn door to see me.

My heart takes one quick skip-beat, but I don't really have time to worry about him, because he walks right up to me and places his head flat against my chest. OK, so there was about ten seconds there where he was roaming free, before he was caught again.

Which is good ... but why was he free in the first place?

"Oh no! Oh Lucas! Come back here!" Sasha, aka fox-faced girl, comes running out of the barn right after Lucas. Her eyes land on me and she startles to a halt. "Oh ..."

"Yeah," I say. "Oh." I scratch Lucas's ear and he sighs and pushes against me. "Do you want to explain this to me?"

"I ... uh ... I'm sorry."

"Well, I hope you're sorry, but I want to know how it happened."

"I ..." She looks at me and blinks twice, quickly. "I noticed his tail was full of shavings, and I know you hate that, so I thought I'd just go in and try to brush them out, and I tied a lead shank across the door so he could look out, but he just *pushed* through it!"

It's an OK explanation for what it covers. It still doesn't tell me why she was in Lucas's small barn, which doesn't house her pony, but I can picture how what she's describing happened.

It's funny how one of the things I resented is her easy confidence around horses. Now I see she's just an eleven-year-old kid. She can handle a horse better than most people, but she's still young – still makes mistakes.

Her weakness makes me like her more which, I'm pretty sure, makes me a terrible person.

She's waiting. I don't think she's breathing. I want her to be scared – a bit. I don't want her to do this again. But it's also the kind of thing I would have done at her age.

"Are you going to get me his halter so he doesn't decide to wander off again?"

"Oh!" She jumps on the spot and whirls back into the barn, emerging again with the halter held out in front of her. "And this," she's also got a lead shank.

Lucas nudges his nose obligingly into the halter, and I click the lead onto it and take him back into the barn. I'm sure he'd walk beside me on his own, but I can't exactly give Sasha hell for letting him loose if I then leave him loose myself.

I click him onto the cross-ties and Sasha stands to the side, looking him up and down. "Is he OK? Is he fine? Oh my God, I would die if anything happened to him ..."

I'm running my hands down each of his legs in turn. "Cut the melodrama, kid. He was loose for about twelve metres." I straighten. "Unless ... is there something else I should know about?"

Her eyes go super-wide and she almost looks little-girl pretty instead of vulpine cunning. "No, I swear, it was just that ..."

"Just what?" Laney steps into the doorway. "Hey girls, what's going on?"

"Hi," I say, and "Hi," Fox-Girl says. Her face has gone extra-white. She looks from me, to Laney, and back again.

"Just what?" Laney asks again.

I shake Lucas's tail. "Just shavings this time. Last time I was here it was full of burrs as well." It's a silly answer, but Laney's question was a superficial one. Even before I'm finished talking she's giving me a *Yeah-Yeah* nod and she's talking.

"Listen, I have great news – the conditioning track is done!"

The, huh, come again, what? I mean, I kind of know what a conditioning track is – even though I've never ridden on one – but I didn't know there was one here.

Sasha, more clued in than me, jumps up and down. "My dad told me it was nearly done!" She turns to me. "My dad's been helping Laney build a conditioning track after work and on weekends – it's partly on our property." She whirls back to Laney. "Does that mean we can try it out?"

"I'll have to double-check with your mom," Laney says. "But you, Em, are good to go if you want to. What do you say?"

I look at Lucas who's doing his best imitation of a dead-quiet, droopy horse right now. Then I remember the panic he injects into me when he does his ever-accelerating trot. Then I remember his instant reaction to 'Whoa!'

"I just started riding him ..."

Laney nods. "You just started schooling him in a ring, which blows his mind. This is running around a trail outside, which he's a total expert at."

I'm not though.

"Remember we made a deal?" Laney says. "You said you'd ride him and I said I'd help? I wouldn't suggest this if I didn't think you could do it."

I shrug. "Yeah. Sure. Why not?" I mean, after all, it's only my funeral.

"Alright!" Laney says. "I'll meet you at the gate in fifteen minutes." She turns to Sasha. "As for you, let's see if we can track down your mother."

"Can I just keep Sasha for two more minutes?" I ask Laney.

She shrugs. "Sure. I'll meet her in the lounge in the main barn."

Sasha watches Laney walk away then turns to me. She's biting her lip.

"Listen," I say to her. "I'm telling you this for your own good. Do not – just don't – go into somebody else's horse's stall unless they ask you to, or you're working for the barn. Got it?"

She nods.

"If anything goes wrong with another person's horse, you do not want to be the last – unauthorized – person who touched that horse. Do you understand?"

"I understand."

"Go find Laney or she'll start to wonder what we're talking about."

Sasha hesitates. "Em ...?"

"Go! I mean it!"

She goes.

***

It's all fine.

No, it's better than fine. It's wonderful.

It's a whole new Lucas. And a whole new me.

The track is the coolest thing I've ever seen – a narrow strip running up one side of the cross-country field, skirting the edge of the distant woods, then returning along the far side of the cross-country. Laney and Sasha's dad have been spending all their spare time removing rocks, chopping out roots, lopping off low-hanging branches, and spreading lots and lots of used, composting bedding on the ground.

"There," Laney says.

"There what?" I ask.

"There. Go. Run."

"How?"

"Just do it. Just go. Give him his head. Have fun."

I stare at her blankly. I am unused to no structure, no rules, no guidelines.

"OK," she says. "If you insist – count a rhythm in your head. That's all – just do that."

Lucas mouths the bit and takes a sideways step.

"See? He wants to go – let him!"

Sasha, sitting beside me on her little paint pony, is wriggling in her saddle, and it's stubborn pride that motivates me to jump out ahead of her. There's no way an eleven-year-old is beating me.

"I ... oh, OK, fine!" I straighten Lucas, so he's facing down the track, and I push my hands forward, lean slightly toward his ears, and whisper, "Alright – go!"

He leaps, too quickly for me to react, which turns out to be a good thing. His first few fast strides are clearly driven by eagerness, as opposed to a desire to bolt, because although he doesn't slow down, he doesn't accelerate either.

It reminds me of the first time I drove a car on the highway. At first a hundred kilometres an hour felt so fast, and I had to push so hard to get there, but by the time I took the exit ramp and had to decelerate to forty, that felt impossibly, draggingly slow.

By the time we've covered a hundred metres, Lucas's speed feels acceptable to me. I remember to breathe. Which reminds me of something else – Laney's words – "count a rhythm in your head." OK. I can do that. I think.

One-two-three-four, one-two-three-four ...

There's a rise ahead and at the same time as Lucas automatically backs off, I automatically chase him forward, trying to hold onto the mental *one-two-three-four* I've established.

On the turn at the top of the field I know we're going to need to be steady and slow, but I'm determined to do it smoothly – maintaining a modified rhythm – before returning to the original beat.

While we run along the edge of the woods – the tree branches breaking the sun's rays and speckling shade across our path, and the two of us – I feel so, so far away. From Laney, from the world, from anybody who can reach me or talk to me.

It's the ultimate in here-and-now living – the wind breezing through Lucas's mane and hitting my face, the drumming of his hooves on ground that sounds near-hollow in places, his muscles sliding under my palm, laid flat on his strong shoulder. This is nothing I've ever done before, so I can't fail at it. This is nothing Lucas has ever done before, so I can't worry that it's all him carrying the two of us through it.

We're trying together – learning together.

Trust. Communication. Fun.

"I love you," I murmur, and he flicks one ear back, then I notice the dip ahead and prepare to balance him, still counting.

***

"Great!" Laney says, as Lucas and I trot, then walk a big circle around her. Sasha, sent off after us, is galloping along the magic forest-side stretch of track – she and Oreo are just a blur against the green of the trees.

Lucas is breathing with an effort, but not blowing. There's still lots of spring in his stride. He's awake. He's pumped.

"How long do you think that took you?" Laney asks.

My brain still has more oxygen in it than normal. Or less; I'm not sure. Either way, I'm lightheaded, with the rhythm of Lucas's stride still ringing through my body. I laugh. "I have no idea!"

Laney crosses her arms. "Well, I'm asking you – how long do you think?"

"Oh." The giddiness flees. She wasn't just asking for the heck of it. I should have known this couldn't be just uncomplicated fun. Couldn't be as simple as "go out and gallop around a field," which – the more I think about it, was all Lucas – I just sat along for the ride.

I frown, shake my head. My heart double-thumps, but not in an elated way. "I really don't know."

She holds up her phone. "It took you just about one minute and forty seconds. Which is, roughly, pre-training speed."

"O-kay ..." I say. *Meaning what?* I don't want to ask.

"I'd like you to do it again at the equivalent of training speed, which should take you about one minute and thirty seconds."

Oh, here we go again, with Laney thinking I actually know something about pacing, and striding, and riding in general. It's true any shows she's seen me ride at I've gotten all my striding right, and hit every spot in any course I've ever jumped, but *that* was all Ava. One hundred per cent. I literally sat on the mare's back, made sure my heels were down, and let her get on with it.

Now I'm supposed to think for me and for this green horse? Now I'm supposed to control our pacing on a conditioning track? To figure out how to shave off ten seconds over three-quarters of a kilometre?

"I can't."

"What do you mean you can't? He can do it easily. He's fit, and it's not a fast pace."

"No – not him – me. *I don't know how to do that.*"

That thing I saw before in Laney appears again. A quickness in her movements – a set in her mouth. She takes a deep breath, then says. "Let's start here. Do you need to go faster, or slower?"

"Faster." *Duh.* How stupid does she think I am? OK, maybe better not to ask that.

"And did you count your rhythm like I suggested?"

Just her mention of it brings the *one-two-three-four* drumming back into my head, like it was on a low volume and I've turned it up. "Yes."

"So, do you think you can use the rhythm to help you get the right time?"

"I ..." *I don't know.* "Maybe?"

"Try."

My frustration is manifesting in clenched fists, tight muscles, and a fidgeting Lucas. I don't think I can do this.

But Sasha is already easing Oreo out of his gallop and I'm not about to debate this in front of her.

Laney glances her way, then says to me. "Quick. Go. I'll start timing you now."

Fine ...

Lucas is just as happy to go this time as he was last time. He's probably thinking running around this track is a good way to escape the neurotic, tense, uncomfortable, riding style I'm too apt to fall into.

Within a few strides the *one-two-three-four* is back in my head. But, wait, no. That's wrong. If I want him to go faster, I need to quicken that rhythm. But not by much. By hardly anything, in fact.

By how much? That's the million-dollar question.

By a breath.

I don't know where the thought comes from, don't know what it even means, but it resonates. Just go a breath faster.

Like the thought has unlocked something stuck in my brain, a new rhythm sets up, which is still four beats, but is just that tiny bit quicker. So little that it almost doesn't seem different, except all of a sudden, Lucas's strides are out of sync with it.

I'm not sure what to use to make the tiny adjustment needed – should it come from leg, hands, voice?

I choose voice, but not by clucking, or urging; I simply speak the words out loud – "One-two-three-four, one-two-three-four ..."

Within a few metres Lucas is matching them.

Unless I've changed my rhythm back to match his stride, in which case, this whole exercise is a hot mess and I give up.

I guess I'll find out at the end, and in the meantime, I might as well enjoy the rest of the trip around the track, with no danger of judgment being passed on me for another minute and ... well I'm not sure how many seconds, but we'll see.

***

While I ease Lucas down through canter, and trot, to walk again, Laney stands, watching, stone-faced.

I'm breathing hard, and after this second trip around Lucas's neck is damp, but he's still eager. Still feels strong. And, for that matter, so do I. This is new to me – this feeling of having worked hard, of being tired, but of feeling stronger for it.

It's nice, and I'm sharing it with Lucas, so I scratch his withers and say, "Good boy!" and decide it doesn't matter what our time was. The gallop was fun, and I'm glad we did it, and we'll be doing it again.

"So?" Laney holds up her phone. "Wanna know?"

So much for our time not mattering. A flutter of butterflies races through my insides. "Yes!"

She peers at the screen. "Well, you did say you didn't know how to pace him. So, I suppose, taking that into account ..." She turns it toward me. "... you totally rocked it!"

1:29.

I blink, then look again. "Really?" I ask.

"Well, I'm not making it up."

"Wow. That's better than I thought."

Laney wags her finger at me. "That," she says. "Is actually pretty darn amazing. I told you to shave ten seconds off ..."

I interrupt, "And I shaved eleven."

She laughs. "Well, considering I can't record tenths of seconds, it was probably somewhere around ten-and-a-half. Which is pretty darn good."

"Yeah?" I ask.

"Yeah," she says. "Obviously it was all my coaching – the rhythm tip – that totally did it for you."

I grin. "Wow, I never knew how lucky I was to have you as a coach until you pointed it out."

"Just ask me anytime – I'm always happy to remind you."

Sasha's coming in from her second round now – her mouth stretched into a grin that looks too big for her small face. Normally I'd think something along the lines of "there's a kid who needs to grow into her smile," but today, right now, there's a feeling pecking, tugging, tweaking at me.

She straightens and drops Oreo to a canter, and says – to me, or Laney, or Oreo, or the world in general – "That was fun!" and I understand why I didn't want to make fun of her.

Because she is me. I am her. We both feel the same way. And so do our horses. And, probably, so does Laney.

And there's an extra-nice feeling that comes from that realization. Belonging. I had no idea how good it felt.

***

I'm heading toward the parking area leaving Lucas, head shoved in a pouf of hay spread in the corner of his stall, eating his way from the inside out. I could hear his munching the whole time I wiped down his tack and swept the aisle.

A non-horse person would probably be convinced Lucas did all the work during our gallop, but my muscles beg to differ. They're tingling in a way that feels satisfying right now, although I'm trying to blank out the possibility of it feeling less rewarding and more painful tomorrow morning.

"Em! Em!" I don't even know how the word of my name change spread to Sasha – Laney must have told her. She's used it faithfully ever since – never once calling me "Mavis," and that makes me willing to stop, turn around, and nearly smile when I say, "Yes?"

She's been running to catch up with me, and her words come out between quick breaths. "Thanks ... *pant* ... for not saying anything to Laney ... *pant* ... about me letting Lucas loose."

I'd almost forgotten about that. I shrug. "Yeah, well, no harm done."

That smile spreads across her face again. It's actually sort of cute. "OK, well thanks."

"OK, well fine." I turn to finish the walk to the car, and realize I'm smiling, too.

I guess this was a good trip to the barn.

Chapter
Twenty-Two

When I get to History, the door's locked. A pile-up of kids masses around the door, mostly heads down, faces lit by the eerie bluish wash cast by their screen lights.

My phone, although I know where it is, has a dead battery, so I stare into middle distance and, one by one, flex and relax my muscles. Between running, and shooting hoops, and galloping Lucas they've been through a lot lately and they ache a bit, but it's that weird ache that can sometimes feel good – like when you snag a hangnail, or push on a bruise. Or, back when I was hardly eating, when I was hungry and the pangs felt like a reward – *you have willpower … you are strong.*

I've worked the muscles of my left leg, and am starting on my right, when I'm snapped to attention by Lucas's booming voice. "Big weekend!"

That's all – "big weekend," along with a big smile shot in my direction – and he keeps walking.

Yeah – big weekend for you and Rory, I think. It's their first basketball tournament of the season, with the first game tonight, games scheduled all day tomorrow, and the play-offs on Sunday.

And big weekend for my mom, who's going to visit my dad. In a flurried combination of excitement at seeing my dad, and guilt for leaving us, she's been filling my in-box with update emails outlining all the never-ending, last-minute changes that come with every basketball tournament. Their second game tomorrow is at 1:00, not 1:30. Tonight's game is at St. Matthew's – not St. Luke's.

Which explains why the weekend is big for me. Lots, and lots, and lots of driving to gyms, and sitting in gyms. Not much driving to the barn.

"Was that Lucas Fielding?" The question is clearly directed at me because it's accompanied by an elbow to my ribs.

I turn to face the girl who asked. I don't really know her. She's one of those "blendy" people – not tall or short, not pretty or ugly, not smart or dumb – I couldn't tell you what colour her eyes are, and even looking at her now, I don't know if I'd call her hair dark blonde or light brown. "Um, yeah," I say. Then I'm seized by a weird need to explain. "He plays basketball with my brother. They have a tournament this weekend."

"Oh, wow," she says. "I wish Lucas would talk about his weekend with me."

My first instinct is to shoot her down – shut her up – tell her Lucas is just a guy, and a sometimes-smelly guy, at that.

But ... but that's not true. Lucas is the nicest guy I know. And funny. And smart. And nice to my brother, which is worth so, so much.

"He's really cute." The girl's words are punctuated by a sigh.

And cute. She's right about that.

"Yeah," I say. "He's pretty great."

And then that's embarrassing enough to make me stride forward, through the crush of phone-captivated students, and reach for the handle of the classroom door. It turns easily and the door swings in.

This is where I'd normally say something like, 'Brains, guys. Use them. Your phones won't open the door for you.'

But Lucas wouldn't. Lucas would hold the door open and sweep his arm wide for everyone to walk in.

So, that's what I do.

On her way by the nondescript girl says, "Thanks."

You should thank Lucas, I think.

***

St. Matthew's is in Dory – the small town nearest to the barn. I drop Rory and Lucas off earlier than the usual thirty minutes they're supposed to arrive before a game and don't even turn the engine off; just accelerate right back out of the parking lot and head to the barn, where I groom half a bag of shavings out of Lucas's tail –*really?* – and go for a running game of tag with him in one of the small, empty paddocks.

Laney comes by in a short break between two private lessons. "Why don't you hop up on him?" she asks.

"I don't have time. I have a basketball game to get back to – I have to leave in about twenty minutes."

"Uh-huh ..." The 'so what?' hangs unsaid in the air.

"I don't have time to tack him up."

She shakes her head. "Yeah, but that's not what I said. I said 'hop up'."

I can't. A quick montage flashes through my head of all the things I've already thought 'I can't' about with Lucas. I can't commit to him. I can't control him. I can't gallop him.

So far, I've been wrong about every single one. So, *can* I ride Lucas bareback?

The problem isn't only that I've never ridden Lucas bareback. The problem is that I've never ridden bareback at all.

I look at Laney. I don't know whether to say it, don't know how to say it ... *Oh, just spit it out* ... "I don't know how to mount him. I've never ridden bareback."

Laney's eyebrows lift. "Well, I guess we'd better fix that quick in a hurry. Nothing could be easier – just bring him over here alongside the fence and climb up, then get on his back."

"Oh ..." Of course. *Stupid again.*

But Laney's not rolling her eyes, or snorting. She's stepped inside to hold Lucas steady against the fence while I clamber up and swing my leg over.

Then – *whoa* – "Cool ..." I breathe it out. He's like a furnace under me. Except a sleek, living furnace made of muscle, and skin, and hair.

Laney laughs. "Awesome, isn't it? Now go for a walk."

She steps away, and I give Lucas a squeeze, and it's amazing how much longer my legs feel – how much farther they reach around his barrel. "He's not really that wide at all, is he?" I ask Laney.

She shakes her head. "No – the saddle adds a lot. And it makes your legs lie differently. It's good to ride your horse bareback – it gives you a different appreciation for how he moves."

No kidding. As Lucas walks, I can feel the lift and push from each leg in turn. Even though I've ridden for years and years, and brought home multiple championships, I still always do a visual check of my diagonal and canter lead. Now, for the first time ever, feeling Lucas's movement this clearly, I have some confidence I might be able to feel those things without looking.

With no bridle on, and me not even thinking about steering, Lucas has decided to follow the perimeter of the fence. Fine with me. It's so much fun to just follow the sway of his walk with my hips, and thread my fingers through his mane, that I don't care where we go, or how fast.

We complete one full circuit and he comes to a stop in front of Laney, who's holding her hand out to him. She squints up at me. "Do you have time to take him around one more time while I ask you a favour?"

"Sure ..." I steer him the other way, and we start walking again, while one or two tiny butterflies rustle around in my stomach. *A favour ... what kind of favour?* Laney keeps pushing me outside my comfort zone, and it keeps being OK, but it's never exactly easy. I ran again last night – another three-point-three-three kilometres – and while I didn't play an hour of pick-up afterwards, and I did do Ellie's stretches, my aching legs still remind me that Laney makes me work hard.

"What is it?" I ask.

"There's an eventing clinic coming up."

If I was a dog the hairs on the back of my neck would be standing up now, because there is no way Lucas or I are ready for an eventing clinic.

"Don't look at me that way!" Laney laughs.

"What way?"

"I know you by now – that's your 'I'm freaking out, I don't want to do this, please don't ask me' look."

"So why are you asking me?"

"Well, if you'd let me finish before you lose it, I'd tell you as part of the bigger eventing clinic, there's a side group being put together as an intro to eventing – for people who want to transition from another discipline, or people who have horses they want to move over – and it would be perfect for you and Lucas, and I've been asked to teach it, and it would be really good for me if you'd ride in it as an example of a horse and rider I'm already working with ..." she takes a deep breath. "... and so at least one person there is guaranteed to be nice to me."

"You?" I ask. "You're worried? Everybody will love you!"

"Well, that's easy for you to say ... you're not the one standing in the middle of the ring putting everything on the line."

I honestly never thought of it before – that Laney could be insecure. That Laney could doubt her own abilities. It makes me want to reassure her. It makes me let down my guard. It makes me say, "Yes, OK. I'll do it."

"Oh!" she says. "That is so, so great! We can talk about all the details when you have more time but it's the weekend after Thanksgiving, and it's on the Saturday, and of course I'll trailer you there, and it's at Stonegate."

I cough. I choke. "Pardon me?"

"It's at Stonegate, so it's not too far, and it's such an amazing opportunity for me since they're more focused on hunter-jumper and I want to focus more on eventing, so maybe we can kind of work together instead of being in competition ..."

Stonegate. Oh, wow. I thought I was done with riding, but now I realize I might have just been done with riding at Stonegate. I don't know if I can go back there.

A month ago, I would have been embarrassed to go back to where I used to be a championship rider, on the back of a free-to-a-good-home green horse who's spent ninety-eight per cent of his career being ridden in Western tack by city people wearing stiff jeans and rubber boots.

Today I'm mortified to think of how they must all see me. A rider carried to success by a horse she never liked that much, or treated very well. A person who said and did anything she wanted, anytime she felt like it.

Somebody riding her daddy's coattails. Someone who would have been nothing without lots of money behind her.

Even if I can't go, I can't tell Laney that right now. She's so happy.

I slide off Lucas's back. "I should get going. But thanks for this."

"Of course. We'll have to do more bareback work in trot and canter."

"Yeah." I'm too freaked out by the Stonegate idea to be freaked out by the idea of trotting and cantering without a saddle.

"Depending how the basketball games go, I'll try to get out another time over the weekend," I tell Laney.

I walk Lucas back to the barn with my palm flat against his shoulder, feeling the now-familiar tensing and releasing of his muscles sliding just under the skin.

Everything with him is so easy. He never knew me any way other than I am right now.

I wish I could do that with everyone – with everything – wish I could have a memory erase machine I could flash at people so they wouldn't remember what a spoiled, entitled brat I used to be.

Lucas reaches out to nudge me. "Oh well, I guess at least I have you."

Chapter
Twenty-Three

I slip in to the gym during the short break between the third and fourth periods.

I catch the little girl next to me on the bleachers staring at my legs and, when I glance down, notice the stripe of dirt and horsehair along the inside of my breeches. So much for all my grooming efforts.

"Dirty, huh?" I ask.

She nods.

"That's from my horse."

Her mouth forms an "O" – "You have a horse?"

The details of my exact arrangement with regards to Lucas fill my head, but she's not interested in them. "Yes. His name's Lucas."

"Like that guy?" She points to the centre of the court where Lucas is taking the tip-off.

"Yup. Like him."

"Cool," she says.

I watch Lucas jump high, stretch his arm higher, and bat the ball into Rory's waiting hands. "Yeah," I say. "Very cool."

***

I'm leaning against the cold cinderblock wall outside the gym. The coach is finishing his post-game wrap-up speech. I know how it goes – what went right and what went wrong. What they should keep doing at tomorrow morning's game, and what he never wants to see them doing again.

I text my dad. **Promised update: they won tonight's game 63 - 58. Rory scored six.**

"Hey, it's really too bad you don't care about the games at all."

It's Lucas; first to be ready as always – shoes changed, bag organized – I tell myself I'm blushing because of the embarrassment that he noticed me jumping up in the stands yelling, "Ro-Ry!"

I use my palms, flat on the glossy thick-painted surface of the walls, to push myself upright. "Yeah, well anyone can get caught up in the excitement of a winning game ... it's possible I even cheered a bit for you."

Lucas raises his eyebrows and points to his own chest. "Really? Me?"

AFTER LUCAS

"Don't get too excited. I think it was when you took that break to tie your shoelaces and you managed a double-knot all by yourself."

"Ooh … that hurts."

This is easy, easy, easy.

Bantering, at this level, with Lucas comes as easily as winning red ribbons did on Ava. She did what I expected her to, I did what she expected me to, it was neat, and tidy, and pretty in a surface way.

And it meant nothing. I sold her – after owning her for three years, after clocking thousands and thousands of kilometres together, after countless times of nearly falling asleep off my step stool while I braided her mane – and I haven't been sad at all, or felt any regret.

I would hate for that to happen with Lucas, but I have no idea how to do things differently.

"What?" he asks. "Why so quiet all of a sudden?"

And, instead of saying, 'You really did have a great game,' or 'I think you're a fantastic friend to Rory,' or, even scarier, 'I think you're a great friend to me,' I blurt out, "Come on, I'll take you guys through the drive-thru on our way home."

Because, of course, French fries and milkshakes are a totally reasonable substitute for true intimacy.

***

Saturday is a day of much basketball. In fact, by the end of the day my left hip has seized up – because there's nothing more ergonomically incorrect than gym bleachers – and there's a weird buzz in my ears; possibly because I've consumed a can of Diet Coke for each game I've watched. Which is five, and an extra can at lunch.

There isn't even any suggestion of a team dinner – the team has back-to-back games at 6:00 and 7:30, and when they win the second one they secure themselves another 8:30 start Sunday morning with a chance to end up playing for gold.

It's another late evening trip through the drive-thru, and after we scarf down our food I let the guys have the shower, and decide I'll run in the morning and shower then.

The phone rings as I'm filling up the sink to wash the few odds and ends of things that got dirty today – the grapefruit knife that can't go in the dishwasher, all of our water bottles – so I answer and put the receiver on speaker, propped on the windowsill. It's my mom and dad, just home from a dinner out in New York. My mom says, "How did that last game go?" In the background my dad says, "Make sure you thank her for the text updates."

"It was really good. Rory's been ..." what I'm thinking is I can't remember the last time Rory had a seizure, but I don't want to jinx it, so I say, "Rory made four three-point shots in a row – it totally changed the momentum of the game. And Lucas was the rebound king. The parents from the other teams all hated him by the end of every game."

As I talk, I rinse an empty bottle, ready to put it in the recycling.

"I've been telling your dad how helpful you've been," My mom says. "I have to be totally honest, and say I'm a little surprised – I expected more complaining and less cooperation, but you've made it easy on me, with him so far away."

I'm wringing out the cloth to wipe the counter, so I almost miss it when she says, "Of course, he might not be away much longer."

"Pardon me?"

"Libby ..." my dad's voice is a warning in the background. "Oh, I shouldn't have said that," my mom says, "Don't say anything to anybody else, but the team's doing so well here, thanks to your dad's hard work, and things aren't good with the team at home. I wouldn't be surprised if they brought him back."

"That's ... um ... great." I hang the cloth over the faucet and pick up the phone, flick it off speaker and stare at my reflection in the dark window – at the furrows across my forehead. "That would be great for you guys."

"For all of us," my mom corrects me. "Things could go back to normal."

"Yeah, to normal. That would be great."

"You sound tired, Mavis."

"Oh, a bit, I guess. It was a long day of sitting on my butt." My voice sounds fake, strained, and it isn't a particularly witty comment, but it satisfies my mom.

She gives a light laugh. "Well, tell the boys we wish them good luck tomorrow, and you get some sleep."

After the call's over, I stare at my face in the window for a while longer. My hair's grown since my dad left. My face is less pointy – it's shaped more like a heart than a triangle. I rub my forehead. It's more than my looks that are different though. I have a new name. I have new interests. I have a new attitude.

I picture everything rewinding. The little blue car I drive every day being replaced by something that seats seven, and is made in Germany. Something with enough horsepower to tow the trailer containing the new show horse I'll be able to have now – glossier, and taller, and even more highly trained than Ava; probably from Florida, instead of just Virginia where we got Ava.

I imagine my mom being home all the time again, with an end to impromptu post-basketball drive-thru dinners, and a return to proper entertaining – cocktails on the back patio, followed by sit-down dinners with well-known power couples.

And she'd also take over basketball again – take if off my hands, I mean – and I'd be free to not try to spend half my life seeking out ingenious routes to avoid traffic on the way to obscure gyms at the height of rush hour.

I sigh, let the water out of the sink, and shake my hands dry before putting the handset back in the cradle.

I'm just tired. And I need to get up early if I'm going to fit a run in before we have to leave.

So, I'd better get to bed.

Chapter Twenty-Four

By the time Lucas and Rory's team wins the gold medal, I have no cuticles left. A 63-62 final score will do that to you. Just because it's not about me, doesn't mean it wasn't exciting to watch.

As the gold medal game starts, the bench beside me creaks and I look over and have one of those disconnected experiences where the wrong person is in the wrong place at the wrong time and I just cannot figure it out. Like if I ran into my grandmother at a Deadmou5 concert. Except this isn't my grandmother. This is forever-legs in clingy black leggings, and a broad smile, and Rapunzel hair braided back in a looks-amazing-and-at-the-same-time-like-I-hardly-care fishtail.

"Ellie!" I say.

She laughs and puts her arm around my shoulders. Gives me a big squeeze and says, "Surprise!"

"Yes! It is."

"Did I miss much?" she asks. "My ringette free skate just ended and I got here as quickly as I could."

Of course she just played ringette. Anybody who just played ringette would look as cool, calm, put-together, and non-sweaty as Ellie does ... or actually no, they never would.

"Wow!" I say. "That is really nice of you ... really."

"Not at all – it's so fun to watch them play, isn't it? You wouldn't be here otherwise."

I don't point out that it's more or less my job to be here, because, she's right. I could drop them off, then take off in the car to do other things. She's right; it *is* fun to watch them. I'm starting to nod when I say, "Whoa ...!" Rory's stolen the ball and is dribbling down the court like a total maniac. The only problem is, dribbling isn't really Rory's forte, and this isn't normally his role, and he's definitely lurching toward the sideline, and as he approaches them his coaches are taking a step back from the bench.

I'm holding my breath, and clenching my fists, and Ellie grabs hold of my arm. "Oh!" I say, and "No!" she adds, then I yell, "Look up, Ror! See Lucas!" and by some miracle, just before he crashes out of bounds, he does see Lucas who is totally open, and he heaves the ball to him, and Lucas gets it and takes it to the net and tosses it up for a sweet, simple lay-up and Ellie and I turn to each other and before I know it I'm letting her hug me and I'm even, a little bit, hugging her back.

She is so easy to like. If Lucas was a mare instead of a gelding, and palomino instead of chestnut, and a human instead of a horse, and a thousand-or-so pounds lighter, he would be Ellie. It might sound like they have a lot of differences, but the two of them do have one huge thing in common. For some reason I can't even begin to understand, they've both taken a shine to me.

Which is crazy, and I don't understand it, but maybe – just like with Lucas – I need to not look a gift horse in the mouth. Just accept Ellie's friendliness.

I readjust my seat – switching to a less-numb part of my butt – take a deep breath and decide to try that.

It's surprisingly more fun to watch the game with Ellie beside me. I feel less like a weirdly out-of-place teenage sister among a sea of coffee-slurping parents and more like ... I don't know like what – like a member of a club. Like Rory, and Lucas, and Ellie, and I are all here together, even if they're playing and we're watching.

"Hey, did I see you running this morning?" Ellie asks.

I've started running early in the morning precisely so nobody will see me, ever, so I freeze for a second when she asks me. "Um ... I don't know. *Did* you see me?"

She nods. "I absolutely saw you. We were on our way to Timmie's before ringette. I banged on my window but you were on the far side of the boulevard."

"Oh," I say. "Yeah. That's near the end of my run."

"Do you usually run early? It's a good time to get it done. Would you want to maybe run together sometime?"

Once upon a time I would have said no, and told her it's because I'm too terrible to ever run with anybody else, and maybe that's still the easiest way out – the way that won't hurt her feelings – but it's not true. The truth is I'm not bad at running – at my kind of running, for my distance, at my pace, alone with my thoughts. And that's why I want to stick to doing it myself for now. But I'm completely unsure of running etiquette ... and friendliness etiquette. Is it OK to say that?

I guess I'll find out. "You know, I think I'm good. I prefer running alone." Ellie blinks, and I rush to add. "But if I did want to run with anyone, I'd totally run with you."

"Cool," she says. "I get that. Sometimes I figure out the plots of my essays in my head while I run.

I exhale before I even realized I was holding my breath. She understands. What a relief. "Yeah. It's like that for me, too."

"So, anyway, what are you up to for the rest of the day?" Ellie asks.

Only half my attention is still with her. Our team scored, but the two points went up for the other team and I'm watching to make sure they're going to fix it. "Oh, I should get out to the barn at some point. I didn't have five minutes yesterday ..." Then, "Good!" as the score gets adjusted.

"I can help!" Ellie says.

"Pardon me?" I'm still thinking of the scoreboard.

"I can drive the guys home after the game and you can head straight to the barn. It's only fair – I know how long you sat inside yesterday."

"Oh ..." I'm going to say 'no' right away. Of course not. That's not how it works – how it works is, I wake up stupidly early, or I get home way too late, I numb my butt on gym bleachers, I yell myself hoarse through tight games, I miss normal mealtimes – and, in return, during the drive home, I get a first-hand play-by-play of the game that just was. I get to hear Lucas and Rory's interpretation of how the game went down. Get to share in their excitement. I'm even getting used to Rory reading stats out loud that I can't possibly hope to understand or remember while I'm concentrating on driving.

But ... I mean, how can I say no? I want to ride today, so now I'll definitely get to. And, Ellie's making a perfectly generous, sensible offer. Plus, let's face it, the guys would probably rather drive home with her. "Um, sure. Yeah. That would be great." I clear my throat and try to sound more convincing. "Thank you."

After the game, Ellie dashes to the bathroom, calling over her shoulder. "I'll be back in a minute. I drank way too much water!"

I find Rory in the hall, bent over the water fountain and punch his arm. "Hey. Nice game."

He mumbles a reply, without pausing in his drinking.

"I don't know if you saw Ellie in the stands? Anyway, she said she'd drive you and Lucas home. That way I can go to the barn."

He does a half-shrug and, between slurps says, "Cool."

OK, good. Normal. Everybody is happy with the arrangement. Fine.

Except it doesn't feel fine to me. I guess it's hard to accept I'm not needed anymore – just like that.

"Um. OK, then. I guess I'll go."

"OK. See you at home later."

"Oh, uh ..." I dig into my pocket. "Here's the rest of the money Mom left for food this weekend. In case you want to pick up some lunch."

Rory takes it. "Cool."

"So." I smooth the now-empty lining of my pocket. "You'll tell Lucas?"

"Yup," he says. "Go! I know you want to."

"Yeah," I say. "You're right. I'm going to go."

And I do.

Chapter
Twenty-Five

A surge of pride hits me when I lead Lucas into the early afternoon sunlight. Even though it's started thickening in the cooler weather, his coat catches the light. His often-brushed tail flows long, thick, and shaving-free. His socks are crisp, his tack is clean ... he looks a million miles from a free-for-the-asking, ex-trail-horse.

I'm pulling down my outside stirrup when I hear a voice. "Oh! Oh-oh-oh! Em! Are you going on a hack? Can I come with you? Will you wait for me?"

Am I going on a hack? Good question. There won't be many more days like this – bright, dry, still warm. Later in the fall there will be many days when wind will drive rain and leaves horizontally across the stable yard, and after that the sun won't make much difference because it will be glinting off sheets of ice and a blanket of snow.

So, yes, I want to hack while I have the chance, but thanks to Ava's deer phobia, and my lack of initiative, I've never actually been out on the trails here. I don't know where they go, or which route will give me a good ride.

"How long are you going to be?" I ask Sasha.

"Five minutes!" she says. "I just need to put his bridle on."

I pretend to think about it. Pretend to hesitate. "Sure, OK. I can wait *if* it only takes five minutes."

"It will! You'll see!" She runs off and I hear her yelling, "Mom! I need you to sweep up after me so I can go straight out with Em!"

* * *

This kid knows all the trails. Thank goodness, because we take one turn, followed by a twist, and I've lost track of where the barn is, where the road is, and once we enter the trees with their branches intertwining overhead it's almost hard to know where the sky is.

When we set out, I told Sasha to go ahead – "Lucas isn't used to leading," I said. Which, I'm pretty sure is true, but also provided me with the tour guide I needed.

There's a benefit I didn't expect to letting her lead the way. For the first time all weekend – for the first time in quite a while, actually – I have no responsibility. I don't have to think, or decide, or plan. I'm letting somebody else plan the route – take me along for the ride – and, even if that someone is eleven years old, it's quite relaxing.

For a long time all I do is watch Lucas's ears, and Oreo's ears in front of him; watch them swivel to catch the sounds of the forest and sometimes swing back to Sasha or to me, as though to say, 'All OK back there? You still with me?'

I also listen to the birds, and the wind in the branches, and the footfalls of the horses, and nothing else at all.

And I feel the sway of Lucas's walk. The subtle changes in his motion when the trail dips down, or rises up, or when he lengthens or shortens a stride to avoid a root, or a rock.

Would I have traded this to be wanted by Rory and Lucas? To be told – 'Hey, you have to come with us. We're used to you driving. It won't be the same without you listening to our endless post-game analysis – especially Rory's stats.'

I don't know – they're different things. I miss that, but I want this, too.

It's probably selfish to want both. If so, I guess I'm selfish.

Anyway, this is what I've got and, as we step out of the woods into a clearing, and the sun hits my face, and Lucas lifts his head and snorts at the cluster of three deer standing just fifty feet to our right – but doesn't freak, just looks, and lets me look – and I lean down and scratch his withers and say, "Good, good boy," I know what I have is pretty great.

Sasha gasps, and the three deer take off, hind legs springing, white tails bobbing and weaving until the disappear into the trees.

"I'm sorry," Sasha says.

"For what?"

"You sighed. My mom sighs when I bug her, so I think I bugged you."

"No," I say. "You didn't bug me."

"Then, what?" She clucks Oreo forward across the clearing and I don't stop Lucas when he falls in stride beside her.

"Nothing." I'm going to leave it at that, but the words, the worry, the churn are in me. There's no way I can talk about this with anybody else. A) It's supposed to be a secret, and b) it will show just how much I haven't changed. Just how selfish I truly am. I sigh again. "OK, listen, if I tell you something can you keep it to yourself?"

Sasha sits up straight, bringing Oreo to a halt, and with her eyes fixed on me recites:

"Cross my heart
and hope to die,
stick a needle in my eye
wait a moment,
I spoke a lie

I never really
wanted to die.
but if I may
and if I might
my heart is open
for tonight
though my lips are sealed
and a promise is true
I won't break my word
my word to you."

"Oh, my ... wow," I say. "Has anyone ever told you you're a weird kid?"

She nods so vigorously her helmet tips over her eyes. "All the time."

"OK, weird kid, here's the deal ..." This time I cluck Lucas forward and it's true – he doesn't like to lead – he waits until Oreo takes a step before moving along beside him. "You know my dad had to move away for work, right?"

Sasha nods again. "Your dad got sent to the small leagues because the team here's tanking and the owner's a jerk, and he blames everyone but himself, and so your family doesn't have much money anymore, and that's why you had to sell Ava."

"*Whoa.* Did your mom tell you that?"

She shakes her head. "My dad. But everyone at the barn knows. They talk about it in the tack room after our lesson."

Great. "Well, anyway – and you can't tell your dad this ..." – I stare at her and she mouths *'my lips are sealed'* – "... they might bring my dad back."

"Oh! Then you'd have lots of money again, and you could buy Ava back, and everything could go back to normal!"

"Yeah, well, that's where the sigh comes in."

I can just make out her brow furrowing under the cap of her helmet. "What do you mean?"

"I've gotten to like how things are these days. I like Lucas." His ears swivel back at the sound of his name – or, at least, I pretend his ears swivel because he's recognizing his name – and I scratch his withers. "Without going into massive detail, I've been busier, and happier, and I've met new people, and done different things, and I like it. I'm afraid if my dad comes back everything will go back to normal – just like you say – and I won't be as happy."

I flip a rogue section of Lucas's mane to the left side of his neck. "And I also know my dad wants to come home, and my mom wants him to as well, so thinking those things means I'm probably still the terrible person I used to be."

Sasha wrinkles her nose. "Am I one of the new people you've met, who you like?"

"Ha! You're cheeky, you know that? Don't push it kid."

She tilts her head to one side. "Well, honestly, I just think you're being pretty dramatic about the whole thing."

"What do you mean?"

"Your dad can come back, and he and your mom can be happy, and you can just not go back to being a terrible person."

I laugh. "You make it sound really easy, but you don't understand – it's more complicated – things will change that I won't have any control over."

She shrugs. "Whatever. Do the things you can control. Keep riding Lucas, and keep being nicer."

"Are you saying I'm not a terrible person anymore?" I ask.

"Ha!" she says. "Don't push it." Then she boots Oreo into a trot and leads the way back to the barn.

Chapter
Twenty-Six

I t would have been nice to come home from riding to
find Lucas shooting hoops with my brother in our
driveway.

But they both already played basketball all weekend,
so it's not surprising that doesn't happen.

It would have been nice if he'd phoned, or texted me
to touch base since I didn't drive him home.

But I didn't phone, or text, him either.

It would have been nice to bump into him at school on
Monday, but even though I make two – or, possibly three
– unnecessary detours to pass his locker, I don't see him.

And since they played wall-to-wall basketball all weekend, Lucas and Rory's coach has cancelled their Monday
practice.

Meaning, I have lots of time to spend at the barn with
Lucas.

We work our way up through what we already know –
a calm and reasonable walk, a forward trot going large –

then move into the things we have more trouble with, like round circles at the trot and a serpentine.

Lucas is getting quite good at bending through his corners, but once the whole exercise becomes a corner – once I want him to hold a sustained bend through a circle, he wobbles. I get more insistent and he tosses his head. His ears flick, and he skitters instead of trotting, and I tense, and brace, and growl, and *this is not going to work.*

There's a thing Lucas and Rory's coach said to one of the assistant coaches, when they got about halfway through a practice and everybody was forgetting their drills, and missing easy baskets, and running the opposite direction from the way they were supposed to go – I liked it so much I jotted it down in my notebook – "Sometimes what you really need to do is start all over again. Go back to your warm-up to reset your attitude and refocus your efforts."

I try it now.

"Walk!" I tell Lucas, and he does that fine. He knows what that means. We long rein around the ring and he stretches out, mouths the bit, and finally gives a deep sigh. I gather the reins, and that's OK, too. He steps into the contact.

I ask for a walk circle and although he loses his focus, and his flexion, a couple of times, he generally sticks to it.

Our hoofprints, if I could distinguish them from the rest of the marks in the sand, would be mostly round and almost even. Which is good enough for me.

So, just do the same thing in trot. "So, just do the same thing in trot," I tell him and cast my mind back to the beginning when I slowed him down by slowing me down. Relaxed breathing, unrushed posting, a mental message that we have all the time in the world to get this done. As soon as he starts to trot it's more collected, better paced for circle work. Then I think of the aids I used in our walk circles and try the exact same ones and it's a million times better.

Maybe not a perfect circle, but a very round oval. And now we're both calm enough that it gets a little better with every try – I figure out that he flattens at the top and leans toward the gate at the bottom, and I anticipate and smooth those issues.

I get a nine-out-of-ten circle on the left rein, switch over to the right and decide I'd give that circle a nine-and-a-half and ride him long around the rein, scratching his withers and giving him lots of "good boy"s.

"Try a serpentine!" It's Laney, foot on the fence.

"Really?" I ask as I trot by. "It's your rule that we quit while we're ahead. Those were good circles."

"They were good circles," she says, "And I think you might just have a crack at a decent serpentine. He's bending, listening, moving forward, and he doesn't look tired. Just try. If it doesn't work, it's on me."

"Alright, it's on you ..." I gather the reins again and Lucas gives a 'what's this?' arch of his neck, but Laney's right – he's listening – so it's on me to give him the right guidance.

Prepare without tensing. I look ahead, plan where the loops should go, exhale a lot, ride mostly off my legs, and, for a first-time try, am very impressed with the seven-out-of-ten serpentine Lucas gives me.

"Great! Now let him walk! I'd give that an eight-out-of-ten!"

I shake my head. "You're being too generous."

She shakes her head. "No, he's never tried it before. Later on, when you're both experts, I'd give it a seven, but for a first try, that was an eight."

Lucas gives a loud, rattling snort and I say, "OK, I'll take an eight."

Laney smiles. "You're both more than ready for the clinic."

A rush of butterflies hits me again. "Oh yeah. The clinic. I said I'd do that, right?"

She points her finger at us. "There is no way you're backing out now. None. I'm not doing it if I don't have a friendly face in the ring with me." Then her smile goes a little crooked and the skin around her eyes crinkles. "And I'll be very happy to have you there, too, Em."

"You!" I lean wide off Lucas's back toward her and she pushes off the fence and skips backward, laughing all the time and I think a few months ago, I could never have imagined joking with a coach this way.

***

As I'm refilling Lucas's water bucket – which is new for me – I used to ride and, yes, groom and tack up, but anything to do with stalls, or feed, or water, well that was someone else's responsibility. Somebody was being paid to take care of my horse and they could darn well do their job.

Today, though, as soon as I see the small swamp Lucas has created in his water bucket – dumping a mouthful of hay into the few inches of water left at the bottom of his bucket – I can't leave it like that.

"So gross!" I tell him as I lift the bucket off the hook to dump it in the long grass at the side of the barn. "This will be better ..." as I pour the fresh water into his swished-out bucket.

I hear a giggle and just see the top of a strawberry blond head peeking over the edge of Lucas's stall boards.

"Sasha? Is that you?"

"Hi!" she says. I flick a few drops of water in her direction and she giggles again. "Oh boy, did it ever work!"

I step aside just in time to let Lucas shove his big greedy muzzle in the clean water – no doubt it will be swampville in there again in about half-an-hour. "What worked?"

"La-ney tricked you!" She sings it more than saying it.

I'm racking my brains. What is she talking about? Did Laney fill Lucas's water bucket up with hay? Am I going to go back to the very dusty car to find Wash me written on the back window? "Laney tricked me, how?"

"After you shut Lucas up during Ava's test ride Laney said, 'Lucas liked her. Wouldn't it be great if I could get her to school him?' But she had to figure out how to make you like him. So, she did stuff like fill his tail up with shavings."

"She what?"

Sasha's nodding. "She noticed you took the burrs out of his forelock that first day. She figured if you saw him again, and he was messy, you might notice him. Not that she had to do much – he is quite a slob on his own – but the next time, before you came to see him, she dumped a bunch of really fluffy, stick shavings in his tail."

"Sasha ..."

Her hazelly-greeny-foxy eyes go wide. "Why would I make that up?"

Good question. It's such a weird thing. How would she even think to make it up?

"Sa-sha!" I've gotten to know Sasha's mom's voice. Peeling her horse-crazy daughter reluctantly away from the barn. Summoning her to homework, or dinner, or piano practice.

"Better go," I tell her.

She sighs. "Yeah. Bye." She runs out then, ten seconds later, is sticking her head back through the door. "Whatever. I'm glad you like Lucas. Because I'm glad you're here. And you wouldn't be here if you didn't like Lucas."

"Sasha!"

"Go!" I say.

She goes and I think about what she's said. If it's true, does it matter? If it's true should I be upset, or happy?

Lucas bumps me with his drippy, hairy, muzzle and I straighten his skewed forelock. "I'm glad I like you, too."

Chapter
Twenty-Seven

It's no surprise both Rory and Lucas have made the school basketball team. They're having their first game in the gym after school today and I'm torn. I want to go. Of course I do. But it stings that nobody's said anything about missing me on Sunday. Rory has spoken to me twice since then – once to ask me to pass the parmesan when he was wolfing down his pasta last night, and this morning when he banged on the bathroom door and told me he wanted in, and I'd been in there for way too long (I'd been in for four minutes).

I have seen Lucas, but it was incredibly brief – when I was already running late for class, I nearly ran into him coming out of a hall I've never seen him in before. It was one of those mutual "Hey!" "Oh!" "Hi!" moments, and it happened right in front of our principal, Mr. Getty, who likes to show how hands-on and engaged he is by standing in the halls during class changes.

"Oh! Hey!" Mr. Getty said, "Better get going to classes or you'll both be late." Then he winked to show how funny he was.

So, even if Lucas missed me terribly, I didn't hear about it then. *Thanks Mr. Getty.*

"We missed you on Sunday!" I turn to see Ellie skipping down the hall to my locker. "I hope you had fun riding, but it would have been better if you were there to listen to Rory's stats after the game."

Before I can say anything, she's threaded her arm through mine. "Come on! The game starts in a few minutes and we have to get good seats."

"Oh, I'm not sure if I'm going. I have homework ..."

"Uh-huh – so do I. Which I'll do in an hour when the game's over. You are not bailing, Em!"

Turns out Ellie's concerns about good seats were a little optimistic – it's early in the season and we're not playing a particularly inspiring team, and apart from immediate family members the bleachers are empty.

Ellie picks us a spot right across from our school's bench and we settle down to watch the end of the warm-up. Lucas sinks a basket, grabs the ball and returns to the end of the line of his teammates. He catches our eye and Ellie hooks her arm around my shoulders, yanks me tight and waves frantically. For a second I think Lucas is going to come say hi, then the coach blows his whistle and they all head to the bench to start the game.

It's not as quick as the competitive games I'm used to watching, but as I get to know the strengths and weaknesses of the other players, it gets more fun.

Ellie stamps, cheers, and whistles. At one point, when both Rory and Lucas are on the bench one pokes the other and they both end up flat on the floor, laughing. "So cute ..." Ellie sighs, then looks at me. "Sorry, you must think I'm silly for thinking he's so cool."

"Just so we're clear here, you mean my brother, right?"

She snorts. "Well, it's not like I mean Lucas!" Then quickly sits up straight. "Not that there's anything wrong with Lucas, of course. I mean, he's great. I mean, if you think he's cool, I totally get that ..."

"I think I'd rather talk about my brother."

"If we're talking about your brother, do you think I'm crazy?"

My instinct is to say, "Looney Tunes!" and tell her all the reasons Rory is much more disgusting, and weirder, and more irritating, than she thinks. Instead I imagine Rory dating Ellie – two nice people who would be kind to each other – and I take a deep breath and say, "No, he's a really, really nice person."

She nods once, firmly. "That's what I think, too." She winks. "*And* he's also really, really hot."

I throw my hands up and wince. "A-a-n-n-d with that comment you have crossed the line."

"I know! I just wanted to rile you up."

We go back to watching the game, but I'm not completely done with our conversation. There's something I still want to ask her, but I'm not sure how.

It makes me itchy, twitchy. It's the first really cool day of the fall, and some kind of temperature inversion seems to have happened, with the gym being hot to start with, then the efforts of twenty-five sweating guys warming it up even more – I'm overheated, and that adds to my irritation.

I shrug out of my cardigan and look at Ellie in what I've come to think of as her fall uniform of leggings and one of those half-athletic, half-stylish yoga-type tops with thumbholes. "Aren't you roasting?"

When she doesn't answer I tug at the sleeve of her top. "Don't you have a tank top underneath? Can't you take that shirt off?"

She hesitates, looks at me for one long second, blinks, then retracts her thumb from the hole. She peels the sleeve back and turns her wrist over, holding it so I can see the milky-white skin, criss-crossed with horizontal ridges.

It takes me a minute to clue in. "Oh ..." and then nothing. My mind is blank. How could someone as great, and funny, and nice, and pretty, and *liked*, as Ellie feel the need to cut herself? I can't even get my mind around it, but I'm pretty sure asking that, right now, in this gym is not the thing to do. "I'm really sorry," I say and then instantly wonder if that's the lamest thing any human being could ever say.

"It's not your fault," she says.

Yup, clearly a very dumb thing for me to say, but I can't think of a way out, so I say, "I know, but I'm sorry it happened."

She smiles, pulls her sleeve back down, leans into me and says, "I *knew* it would be OK to show you."

Oh. Ellie's already yelling, "Come *on*, ref! Traveling – call it!" I don't know what, exactly, just happened here, but it seems like I did something right.

It gives me a micro-second burst of courage, enough to blurt out the question I've been sitting on. "Ellie? You liking Rory – is that why you've been hanging out with me lately?"

I thought it was going to be hard to ask the question, but it's even harder to just sit, and not add anything, and wait for her answer.

"Oh, wow, Em. I can see why you'd think that. And, I mean, obviously you two are tied up together in my mind. I first noticed Rory back when I was in your class in grade school – I thought he was such a cool big brother even then. I can't take the idea of you away from him, or him away from you, but I'll tell you this one hundred per cent for sure, I don't hang out with people I don't like."

"So, you like me?"

She grins. "I'm hanging out with you."

My phone vibrates, and I know what it is – a reminder from my mom that I have to get home to put the dinner she prepared in the oven at 5:00. There are days when I would have sighed, and deleted the message, and figured there was no harm in pushing 5:00 back to 5:30. Right now, though, I could use some fresh air and some time to think.

I gather my things and tell Ellie, "I've got to get going – that was my mom reminding me to start dinner."

"Oh!" she says. "OK. I guess Rory can tell you the final score anyway."

As I stand she says, "Hey, Em?"

"Yeah?"

"Thanks for coming." Then she tugs at her sleeve. "Thanks for everything."

"Um, yeah," I say. "Of course."

As I walk home, kicking my feet through curled-up skiffs of red, and orange, and yellow leaves, I think of Ellie.

Ellie is, I think, my friend. It's amazing the power that simple thought has to make me simultaneously happy and bring me nearly to tears.

One of the reasons I know Ellie is my friend is that she shares things with me. Like her cutting. Like having a crush on my brother.

So, maybe I should tell Ellie how I feel about Lucas. That feels scary. It could be embarrassing. I'm not sure ...

Following that line of argument, maybe I should tell Lucas how I feel about him. *Whoa*, instant twist of panic through my gut.

By comparison, telling Ellie seems much easier.

I adjust my backpack and decide to put that conversation on my to-do list.

No need to rush on that. I have far more important things to do.

Like get home in four minutes to put tonight's dinner in the oven.

***

When the phone rings, I'm squinting at my mom's hand-writing, trying to figure out if the note she left says the oven should be heated to three-fifty or three-sixty. I'm frustrated, irritated, and ready to let it go to voicemail when the ring shifts to the warble of a number entered in our directory. Better answer ... or at least check who's calling.

It's Laney.

My body goes cold, then rushes hot. The way most barns work is you really don't have to call them, or they you – ever. When you spend six days a week at a place, it's easy to talk to people when you see them, or leave a note, or a cheque in a locker or on a bulletin board.

The only time I've ever received a call from my barn was in my early days of riding at Stonegate to tell us my pony at the time – the fun and funky little Pushkin – had somehow hooked her blanket onto the gate, then gone ballistic freeing herself. There was some blood, and some swelling, and they'd called the vet and wondered if we wanted to be there for the exam.

So now I fumble to press "talk" and almost yell, "Laney! Is Lucas OK?"

I love him. So much. It hits me just like that.

If Lucas isn't OK, I won't be OK. I love that big-bummed, dirty-tailed, non-pedigreed, weirdly energetic, barely trained trail horse more than I've ever loved any sleek, conditioned, push-button, red-ribbon-winning machine I've owned before.

I love him, and he's not mine, and the thought of him being hurt scares me to my core.

"Whoa! He's totally fine. I didn't mean to freak you out."

"He's fine?"

"He's great. Which is what I wanted to talk to you about."

"The clinic," I say.

"Who ever said you were slow on the uptake?"

My voice sharpens. "Who did?"

"Nobody did, ever, Em. It was a joke." Laney sighs. "You are, sometimes, a wee bit prickly though."

Understatement of the century.

"If only you knew ..." I say. "Sorry. The clinic."

"I noticed you didn't fill out the registration form I left clipped to the stall door."

It's not a question, so I don't answer.

"Not the last time you were here, or the time before," she continues.

I punch three-five-oh, then "start" into the oven, take a deep breath, and think of telling her I'm nervous, I'm not sure, maybe I'm not ready, maybe Lucas isn't ready.

But Laney has a pretty good bullshit-meter. So, I tell the truth. "Here's the thing – I don't think I'm the world's most-loved person at Stonegate. It's possible I left some bad vibes behind me there and I'm feeling just a tiny bit awkward about going back."

"Bad vibes?"

"Let's just say a lot of people there were probably pretty glad to see the back of me, and there's a good chance if I hadn't pulled out, they might have asked me to go."

"Oh," Laney says.

"Aren't you going to ask why – what I did?"

"Em, how stupid do you think I am?"

"You knew?"

"Let's just say the horse world is a small one. Let's just say I had a hint you might be less-than-easily-coachable."

"And you still coached me?"

"Well, your parents paid for your lessons."

"OK, now I feel warm and fuzzy."

"Ha!" Laney laughs. "Of all the things you are, I didn't think self-pitying was one of them. Anyway, it's really not important what I'd heard about you before – what's important is what I'm offering you now. A great opportunity. One you've earned. One you're completely up to. And we'll have each other's backs over there at big, bad, scary, show-central Stonegate. You, and me against the world."

I quite like the idea of being against the world with Laney. Although I don't want to be against the whole world. Not Rory, or Lucas, or Ellie. I guess not my mom and dad, and probably, not even Grace. Maybe, if I'd tried to get to know her, I would have found out annoyingly perfect Grace was actually quite a bit like Ellie.

"You, and me, and Lucas?"

Laney laughs. "Yes, Lucas, too." Then she yawns. "OK, then ..." Her days are long, and they start early. I'm sure she has a dozen things to do before she gets to have dinner, or go to bed. I should let her go.

"Wait!"

"What?"

"Just ... what made you go from only coaching me because my parents paid for lessons, to offering me Lucas?"

She laughs again. "Oh, Em. You don't mind looking a gift horse in the mouth, do you?" She yawns again. "I guess it was partially that I saw something in you – call it a spark, or potential, or whatever you like ..."

My chest puffs up.

"... and partially that every other half-decent rider already had their own horse to school and Lucas really, really needed some attention."

Whoosh! The air whistles out of my inflated chest.

"But the important thing is, I'm glad I gave you the chance, Em. So just focus on that – it doesn't really matter what happened before, or exactly how we got here, we're here and it's all good."

***

Face washed, teeth brushed, I'm heading down the hall to my bedroom when I pass Rory's open door. He's lying on his back, tossing a hacky sack in the air. *Up-down-up-down* – the repetitive slapping noise drives me crazy when he's bugging me, but mostly I've come to like it. It's a sign my brother is home, thinking, relaxed. It's a sign there are no bigger problems in this world, because when things are seriously wrong, you don't lie around tossing a hacky sack.

He catches me looking and, still tossing the hacky sack, says, "Yes?"

It blurts out of me before I have time to wonder if it's a good idea, or a bad idea, or what Ellie would think, or where my loyalties should lie. "What do you think of Ellie?"

My brother snatches his hacky sack out of mid-air and holds it tightly in his fist. Which, alone, is a big sign but his cheeks also rush a blotchy red.

I square my feet and my shoulders, ready for verbal battle. He'll deny, and I'll see he's embarrassed but I'll push anyway. I've done it before – when his acne flared, when he got an unexpected low mark on a Chemistry test, when he was having trouble mastering the trombone – *poke, goad, tease* until his temper flares and he yells at me, or whips the hacky sack at the wall. My mom might have to put down her tea and head for the stairs warning, "I've just paused Netflix … if I were you guys I'd sort this out before I get all the way upstairs!"

He catches me completely off guard when he says, "What do you think of Lucas?"

Oh, the blotchy red cheeks that run in our family – I feel their bloom on my own face. *Shit.*

He nods, once. "Thought so."

It's my turn to deny, but just like my brother did, I try something different. "You could do worse, you know."

"You could too."

He smiles, starts tossing the hacky sack again. "Well, it's good we got that settled. Make sure you invite me to the wedding."

"Maybe we should have a double wedding."

Up-down-up-down, slap-slap-slap-slap. "Sure, let's discuss that. Just not tonight."

"OK," I say. "Good-night, then."

"'Night."

I leave my door open so I can fall asleep to the rhythm of Rory's hacky sack.

Chapter
Twenty-Eight

Because my dad flies home for Thanksgiving on Thursday I don't ride, and Rory doesn't play basketball. My mom and my brother and I go to the airport together, and as we drive away – heading to a local restaurant for dinner – it feels weird to have all four members of our family in the car at the same time.

Weird, but quite nice.

My mom smiles, but doesn't say much while Rory and my dad talk about basketball (mostly) and hockey (a bit) and it's fine with me because, unlike in previous years, I can follow everything they're saying.

In the middle of the conversation my dad stops and says, "Of course, I wouldn't be so up-to-date on all this if it wasn't for Mavis's texts."

It's nice to be acknowledged but so, so strange to hear that old name said out loud. Rory and I are both quiet for a few seconds, that end up feeling like long minutes, and my dad says, "What? What did I say wrong?"

"It's just she goes by 'Em' these days." Rory says, and turns out when he says it, it doesn't sound huge, or weird – it just sounds factual.

"Do you?" my dad asks, at the same time as my mom says, "You do?"

I shrug. "It just feels more like me."

My mom opens her mouth, and my dad cuts in, "Well, I guess that's understandable *Elizabeth* – isn't it?"

Elizabeth. I suppose I knew, somewhere in the back of my mind that was my mom's full name, but she's so completely and totally a "Libby" that it sounds really weird to me.

Her mouth snaps shut again, and she straightens her shoulders and says, "So, Rory and Em, are you ordering dessert?"

***

We come home to dishes piled in the sink. We didn't even eat at home, but it's amazing how many odds and ends of containers and water bottles pile up over the course of the day.

My mom's been working long hours, and even her smiles at having my dad home don't mask the dark circles under her eyes. "Aren't you going to bed?" I ask.

"In a minute," she says. "I don't want to leave the kitchen looking like this."

Instead of arguing with her – pointing out it will all still be there in the morning – I say, "You go ahead. I'll do it."

She blinks, twice, and for a second I wonder if she's going to cry. Talk about awkward and horrible. She just shakes her head, though, and says, "How about you wipe down the counters, and I'll wash the dishes, and we'll be done in no time."

It's when my back is turned to her – when I'm reaching to wipe the crumbs out of the deepest corner of the counter, that she clears her throat. "Your name," she says. "I've always felt badly about that."

I freeze. It's hard to imagine my matter-of-fact, forward-marching mother feeling badly about something from the past. "About what, exactly?" I ask.

"Well, more than just your name, really. About sending you to live away from us." There's a quiver in her voice as she says, "Can you please look at me when I tell you this? It's long overdue, and I should probably just get it out."

I don't want to turn. I don't want to meet her eyes. But *long overdue*, and *just getting it out*, sound about right, so I turn.

She pours rinse water out of a bottle and settles it in the dish drainer then looks at me full-on. "At the time, it seemed like the right thing to do for everybody. We didn't know what was wrong with Rory. We didn't know how sick he'd get. We did know we were going to be taking turns sleeping at the children's hospital for a long, long time, and we knew we hardly had any spare time, and we'd already had to call in babysitters, and neighbours, and once your dad's executive assistant, to look after you on short notice." She takes a deep breath. "It felt wrong, and chaotic, and not fair to you, so when your Aunt Mavis offered to have you go stay with them, that felt right. It felt like it would be a better environment for you. Calmer. It was right at the beginning of the school year, so you could just do a year there and we figured by Christmas, or the end of the school year, we'd know more about Rory and have things under control, and you could come back."

I thought I didn't remember this, just like I didn't remember Ellie's long-ago birthday party, but it turns out the details might be hazy, but my body remembers.

My jaw clenches. My shoulders tense.

And there are some details I do remember. Like I wasn't allowed to come to breakfast in my pyjamas – I had to get dressed every morning before coming downstairs. Like the time I flooded the bathroom because I left the shower curtain outside the tub – at our house the showers had glass doors. Like how big, and old my cousins seemed – breezing in and out of the house between university classes and jobs – they were nice to me, but were never there. I was the only nine-year-old in the house. I was the only nine-year-old who had been in that house for a long, long time, and you could feel it. It was a house for older, more serious people.

It made me more serious. It turned me from an Em into a Mavis.

I was even younger than Sasha. Wow, that seems so, so young.

"I never felt at home there." I say it half to myself, as the memories come back, but my mom blinks and wipes at her eyes.

"I'm so sorry ... Em. Looking back, I can see it wasn't the right decision, but ..."

And I get it – I do – now that she's explained. I get that my parents didn't know what was happening to Rory, or to them, or to our family, and they probably weren't getting very much sleep, and sending me to stay with my Aunt Mavis – who is a perfectly nice woman likely seemed like a sensible idea.

But can I articulate any of that? Not a chance. The only thing that comes out of my mouth is: "My name ..."

"I know, Em. Your dad had such a small family – just his older sister, and he looked up to her so much; she helped raise him – so I agreed to name you after her, but on the condition that you'd always be called 'Em' not

'Mavis'. Of course, we always called you 'Mavis' when she was around, then when you went to live there, that's what she called you, and I don't know why, but it stuck."

She drops her eyes away from me, and that suits me fine. She wrings out the dish cloth, before adding. "I guess it seemed like a small thing to let go. Not a battle worth fighting. And, of course, your dad liked the name, so it didn't bother him at all ..." She hangs the cloth over the faucet and turns to face me head on. "But I realize now, of course, that you were losing things too, and I shouldn't have made you lose your name."

I lost so much more, I want to say. It wasn't just my name, it was me. I wasn't the same after that ... But, I guess none of us were the same after that. Sometimes it's hard to know what other people are going through.

I think Laney's tough and confident, but she's worried about teaching at Stonegate.

Ellie seems perfect, but she used to cut herself, and her yen for my brother is – so far – unrequited.

Earlier in the year one of Rory's teammates looked at me and asked Rory, "Why's your sister always here? Why don't you just drive yourself?" I'm sure he's not the only one who has no clue why a teenage guy gets driven everywhere by his sister.

The stay with my Aunt Mavis was a long time ago, and I can't really figure out what good sulking about it would do now.

I toss the cloth I've been using into the sink behind my mom. "Listen," I say. "I'll make you a deal. If you never – like not ever – call me Mavis ever again, we can forget about the whole thing."

"I don't think it's that easy to forget about such a big thing," my mom says.

"I've had some very good advice recently," I say. "Wanna hear it?"

"Sure."

"Don't look a gift horse in the mouth."

My mom gives a snorting surprised laugh. "That's not super-original advice."

"But does it apply?"

"Fine," she says. "Yes. Deal. And thanks for your help. Tonight, and for the last while. I appreciate it, *Em*."

I smile. "That's a good start. Now let's just keep it up."

***

My dad spends Friday in meetings. He's gone early, and home late, and when he gets back he's whistling. He takes my mom out for dinner at a restaurant far too swishy for Rory and me to go, and I spend the evening working through our Bio lab with Ellie who Skypes me from her grandparents' house in Peterborough.

"What's Rory doing?" she asks at one point. "He must be at loose ends with no basketball this weekend."

"Playing endless and uninterrupted NBA on the PlayStation."

She laughs. "Oh, so he's pretty much in heaven."

"Yeah." I'm tempted to ask her if she knows what Lucas is doing for Thanksgiving; it feels like forever since I've seen him. He was sick at the beginning of the week, so he missed practice, then Rory didn't go to the week's second practice. But even if Ellie knows what Lucas is doing it doesn't really matter. He's either around, in which case he'll probably come by and see Rory at some point, or if he's out of town visiting family I won't see him. Asking Ellie won't change that.

Then again ... she trusted me. "Speaking of basketball, I haven't seen Lucas all week. Do you know what's up?"

"Yeah, his dad asked me to put their recycling out for them because they were leaving a day early to go see his grandmother in Windsor. It's such a long drive, they usually make it an extra-long weekend when they go there."

Oh. I didn't know Lucas's grandmother lived in Windsor. It makes me realize how much I don't know about him. Gives me a huge pang of insecurity. I like him based on what? A few drives to basketball. He has this whole other life that has nothing to do with me. I'm glad I haven't told Ellie I like him.

"Em?"

"What? Yeah?"

"You went quiet on me there."

"Sorry. Rory just yelled. I think he won his completely fake NBA game."

"Em?"

"Yeah?"

"I'm pretty sure Lucas would rather be at home than in Windsor."

"What makes you say that?"

"Because I'd rather be at home than in Peterborough, and I think Lucas and I have the same motivation for liking to be at home."

"Lucas has a crush on Rory?"

"Em ... stop."

She's so nice to me and it's still hard for me to get my head around it. If I don't want her to stop, maybe I should reciprocate. "OK, OK," I say. "I also have that motivation."

"Admitting it is the first step," Ellie says. "Nice work. I'm proud of you."

"Yeah, although it is a bit embarrassing to have a crush on my own brother."

"If I was there, I'd hit you."

"Well, see? Now I'm glad you're in Peterborough."

***

Later, as I'm getting myself a drink of water before bed, Rory pushes my glass out of the way and asks, "How's Ellie?"

"Good," I say. "We got our whole lab done, then somehow we end up on Skype for another half-hour."

Rory puts one finger on his nose and uses his other hand, sloshing glass and all, to point at me. "That, my sister, is what's generally referred to as 'having a friend.' It's nice that you're trying it."

"Hey!" I yell after him as he walks away. He doesn't turn around and I guess that's OK since, come to think of it, he didn't say anything I should be mad at him for.

**

Suddenly I can't drive. I've been driving all over the city and the countryside in all kinds of approaching-winter-weather conditions, usually with two sometimes-loud, sometimes-distracting passengers, and I've been solid. But with my quiet, polite father in the passenger seat the whole car feels unfamiliar.

I take exaggerated care with my stops, turn signals, and lane changes. It's only after I've (very carefully) merged onto the highway, and we're spinning along with the speed of traffic, that my dad starts talking, and with that distraction driving resumes being the normal, natural activity it normally is for me.

"It will be official next week," my dad says. "They're asking me to come back and, actually, I'll be getting a promotion."

"That's great," I say. "You must be really happy."

"I am," he says. "But, as much as I thought I didn't want to go to New York, and as much as I missed your mom – and you guys – while I was there, I learned quite a bit in a very short time."

"Me too," I say.

He shifts in his seat. "About you, Mavis ... I mean, Em ... I think I owe you an apology."

I change lanes, smoothly, expertly, like a driving pro. "In what way?"

"I always understood Rory, playing basketball, it was a sport I *got*. And he was sick, so we always worried about him. But you; well I never really understood riding, and you were fine – strong, actually, and tough – and I think I just let paying for your riding be my contribution."

It's funny that I used to feel that way. Used to blame them. Now I can see, though, how prickly I was. How hard I made it for them to be involved – let's face it; I wouldn't have wanted to hang out with the old me. I feel like I should speak up but my dad keeps going.

"It's been an eye-opener how you've stepped up this fall. Without you driving Rory couldn't have played competitive basketball – and I think it's been really good for him – without you it would have all fallen on your mom, and she couldn't have done it. And she says Rory hasn't missed one practice, or game, and you've never complained." He pauses. "I'm a little embarrassed to admit it's more than I expected from you."

I've had very little practice accepting praise which is partly, I admit, my own fault for not earning that much of it. Because I'm not sure what else to say, I tell the truth. "I liked doing it. It was fun."

"Yes, well, speaking of fun, now I think it's time for us to offer you some fun. Your mother and I have talked about it and we can't take all your new responsibilities off your hands. My new position will require considerable travel, and your mother's found she likes her job – she's going to scale back hours – but she's going to keep working. Until Rory is seizure-free for a year, and can get his license, we may need you to help with driving, but certainly not as much as this year."

"I don't mind ..." I say.

My dad holds up his hand. "The thing is, your mother and I weren't always sure how much you rode because it was *there*, versus you actually loving it, but since you've shown your commitment by continuing to go to the barn even when you don't have a nice horse to ride, and even when you aren't showing every weekend, we think once my new job is formalized you should look for another horse. And, if you like, we can move you back to a more established showing barn.

He's quiet now, so I know it's my turn to respond. "I ..." How do I say what I'm thinking without seeming ungrateful? How do I explain what I've come to love about riding – what took me such a long time to learn – to somebody who barely understands it in the first place?

The indicator's tick-tocking and we're turning onto the stable drive. "You said you never really understood riding, Dad – maybe I can show you. Why don't you just wait and see?"

***

It's early when we get to the barn. So early that Laney's still throwing down hay for the morning feed.

"Hi!" I yell up through the hatch, and "Hey!" she yells back down, then adds, "Can you bring the whole herd in, please? By the time you get them in I'll have the last stalls hayed."

"Of course." I glance at my dad, standing next to me, looking like he'd be much more comfortable by the bench at a hockey rink. "My dad's here!" I yell.

Laney's voice drifts down, "Hi, Mr. McElvoy! I'll see you when I get down."

"Come on," I tell him and lead the way through the main barn with me checking that all the herd horses' stall doors are open. "Could you just pull that one back a little more?" I ask my dad, while I bend to pick up a halter that's fallen into the aisle.

We walk through the wide loafing area that serves as the transition between the barn and the field. It's empty except for shavings bags stacked on pallets against one wall. While the barn is weathertight and shipshape, this space is built of reclaimed board from the original barn that stood on this property. The floor is dirt and there are tiny gaps where the boards join, and in some of the wood itself. In the winter, I can imagine skiffs of snow will be drifting through them just a few weeks from now. Today, morning sun filters through, highlighting dust motes floating in the air.

Although I've helped Laney bring the herd in a couple of times before, I've never paid much attention to how this place looks. I wonder how my dad sees it. I've come to love the quiet dimness infused with the scent of horse and earth, but to him it might seem just dirty and dark.

I grab hold of the big sliding barn door at the end and haul at it until it starts rolling in its tracks, and light floods in. "Better?" I ask.

"It's fine," my dad says. "It's all fine."

We're at the top of a rise. The field is spread below – some of it open meadow, the rest treed.

"Where are the horses?" my dad asks.

"Just wait and see ..." I cup my hands around my mouth, take a deep breath, and holler, "C'mo-o-o-n ...!" I hope they'll come when it's just me calling, without Laney. It'll be mortifying if I just holler into the country-side and nothing happens.

I turn to my dad. "Why don't you help me?"

He hesitates, then lifts his hands to his mouth, too.

"C'mon," I say, first to him, then turning to the big field repeat, "C'mo-o-o-n ...!"

I'm starting to wonder whether I'm going to have to grab a bucket of grain and give it a good shake, when the first shapes start appearing out of the trees.

One, then two, heads low, walking steadily. Then a third and a fourth, and soon there's a dozen, with more coming.

A gelding at the back breaks into a trot and every horse he passes jumps into a trot as well.

My eye falls on the big-boned chestnut I've been look-ing for, just joining the edge of the group, and my heart makes this funny lifting, floating, swelling sensation. "Lucas!" I laugh.

I turn to my dad, "That's him – my – well the horse I've been riding." Lucas tosses his head, and bucks, then breaks into a canter. "Monkey ..." I say.

The younger, greener horses canter beside him. The old campaigners let them go, sticking to their steady trot as they approach the hill up to the barn.

They come in a rumble – up the rise and around the corner and they're facing us, head on. They're kicking up dust and we can hear and feel their hooves on the ground.

"What ...?" my dad starts to ask, and I say, "It's OK. Just stand where you are. They'll go right past."

They do – a blur of bay and grey, chestnut and paint, and one palomino – sweeping by just a couple of feet from us; a living whirl of energy and muscle that we can see, smell, hear, and that's close enough to reach out and touch.

As we listen their hooves go from thudding to clomping as they make the transition from the dirt to the cement floor.

One stops, though. Lucas. He halts right in front of me and reaches out his nose, as though to say, 'Hey, you're here. Cool.'

I straighten his forelock and turn to face my dad. He looks straight at me, blinks twice, then shakes his head and says, "Well, that was life-changing."

And I think, just maybe, he's right.

Chapter Twenty-Nine

Laney was right; by the time my dad and I follow the final stragglers into the barn, she's got the hay distributed and we walk through the barn shutting each horse in his or her stall.

"Are they all in the right place?" my dad asks.

"Yup – today they are," Laney says.

"Do they ever get it wrong?"

"Maybe, if they've just been moved to a new stall, but not for long."

"That is really quite incredible," he says.

He's also impressed that Lucas follows me the whole time, including out of the big barn and across the stable yard to his own small barn.

"He's like a dog," my dad says.

"A big dog."

I shouldn't be letting Lucas follow me like this – loose in the yard with the unsnapped lead coiled in my hand – but it feels so nice to have my dad's attention, I can't resist.

**

I'm a little nervous to have my dad watching – especially after my "wait and see" proclamation – but it helps that Lucas and I have a routine now.

"Hey, Em!" Sasha's sharp little face and peppy voice is starting to feel like part of our routine, too.

There's no shaking her, so in the spirit of "if-you-can't-beat-'em-join-'em," I say, "Hey Sasha, this is my dad. He doesn't know much about riding, so maybe you can tell him what we're doing."

I'm not sure if my dad's going to love her, or hate her, but Sasha's part of the deal so it is what it is.

Better than a routine; Lucas and I have an agreement. I will be subtle and gentle and understated with my aids, and he will keep his responses within the realm of normalcy.

If I avoid the clutch and grab, he'll avoid the zip and zoom.

Because of that, by the time Laney appears, we've walked and trotted on both reins, including trot circles spiraling in from twenty to fifteen metres, then back out again. It's all been accomplished at a steady pace, and Lucas has been bending – more or less – which is to say, more on his left side, less on his right.

The way I become aware of Laney's presence is when she says, "How about the canter?"

I know why she's asking. She's asking because a) the clinic is a WTC clinic, b) our "C" (canter) needs a lot of work, c) I've been avoiding it.

"Oh, hello Laney," I say. "Good morning, Laney." "I'm fine, Laney – how are you?"

"I take it that means you haven't cantered yet."

"I was getting there." *His trot is so nice now. The canter just ruins everything.* I don't want my dad to see us fall apart. "It was next on my list."

"Perfect timing, then. Get on a trot circle around me."

I steer Lucas in a round trajectory with Laney at the centre, but it's not a forward, bending, well-shaped circle like before. I'm bracing for our race into canter, where Lucas trots faster than the standardbreds at the racetrack until he eventually does some weird hop and throws all four legs around and lands in a canter that's on the wrong lead fifty per cent of the time, and disunited twenty-five per cent of the time. And my twenty-five per cent success rate only means he's cantering on the right lead – not that he's doing it well – he still charges around with his head in the air, stiff as a board.

"Em! Exhale. Relax from your brain down, follow his mouth, sink your heels down – back to basics, ride the way you know how to."

Grrr ...

"Say it out loud!" Laney yells.

"Grrr!"

With the grrr goes breath and tension, and Lucas instantly relaxes and we're on a proper, flexed, balanced, impulsion-laden circle.

I laugh. "Who knew that would work?"

"I did! And this will too – spiral in."

I go back to the warm-up exercise we've already done successfully and I experience one of those moments of lovely perfection. Of flow and ease. Of cooperation between me and my horse.

"Leg yield out!" Laney calls, and I do – gradually – more a function of thinking our way out than of lurching. I ask, Lucas steps, the circle gets wider, he stays flexed ... it's nice.

"... aaand ... outside leg back, eyes up, exhale, and canter!"

Oh! Really? Just like that?

Just like that – "Don't hunch, sit tall, chest forward, follow with your hips ..." – I know these things, but it helps to have Laney reminding me, and I do everything she's saying as well as I can, and Lucas steps into the sweetest, softest transition I've ever felt.

"No! Way!"

"Good!" she yells, "Go large! Keep the rhythm – just like on the galloping track."

We rock around the ring in the steadiest three-beat rhythm ever, and this is good enough for me. This is fulfilling on its own. This is sweet satisfaction.

When I bring him down to a forward walk, through the trot, Sasha whispers from her spot on the fence, "That was so, so good, Em."

I grin. "It was. He was," I agree.

"That was really good ..." I hear Sasha starting to explain to my dad, and I wonder how he's enjoying his running commentary. But I only wonder for a minute, because this is about me and my horse. Not anything else. Not anyone else.

***

We do it once on the other rein and Laney says, "Great, walk him." She steps back and looks us back to front, up and down. "What do you think?"

I hesitate. "I think that was amazing. But ..."

"But what?"

"Is it enough for the clinic? We're not even doing canter circles yet."

"It's enough. It's a beginner clinic." She laughs. "You can't be perfect going into the clinic – you need something to work on." More seriously, she adds. "But it's up to you. You have to be confident enough to do it."

Lucas gives a long, snorting exhale, and stretches his head longer and lower, and I remember that moment of elation when he stepped so nicely into his correct lead canter, and I say, "Yes. Fine. What the heck. We can do it."

"Yay!" Sasha yells from the fence and I turn around to catch my dad shrugging his shoulders. "I'm not sure what everyone's so happy about, but it sounds good."

Taking her teaching role seriously, Sasha turns to my dad and says, "Oh! There's this clinic coming up, which Laney wants Em to ride in, and a clinic is ..." I circle away and leave her to do my explaining for me.

Laney looks at her watch and yelps, "Yikes! I have a lesson to teach. Gotta run!" On her way out of the ring she calls back, "Why don't you untack him and let him roll?"

There's just one problem with that. Once all his tack is off, and Sasha's holding his bridle over her shoulder, with his saddle balanced on the fence, Lucas won't roll, or even lie down.

He just stands, with his head pressed against my chest, ears flicking as I tell him what a silly, silly boy he is.

I shrug. "Maybe no roll after all."

Sasha calls out, "Lie down with him!"

No. That's crazy. It's ridiculous. I'd look like a fool.

"Now that is something I'd like to see," says my dad and I figure it never hurt anyone to look a little foolish.

"If I get kicked in the head, it's one hundred per cent your fault," I tell Sasha, then I step back from Lucas, paw the ground a couple of times – what the hell; if I'm going to do this, I might as well commit – and drop to my knees.

He lowers his head and gives a long, rattling snort.

I collapse on my side then roll right over, and feeling really dumb, and very sandy, struggle to my elbows just in time to see the big gelding also drop to his knees, and then right down into the sand, and roll, and roll, and roll – the whole thing punctuated by grunts and groans, and finished with a big scramble to his feet and a vigorous shake.

Sasha dashes into the ring, giggling, and starts to whack at my breeches.

"What are you doing?" I ask.

"Cleaning you off!" Then Lucas reaches out and gives me a big shove with his nose, and I'm laughing and Sasha's laughing, and Lucas is following us around, and my poor dad is standing at the gate watching it all. "Is this what it's always like here?" he asks.

"Um, no – not exactly," I say.

"But it's always fun!" Sasha says. "You should come more often."

"Oh yeah?" he asks.

"Oh yeah!" she says, and runs forward to link her arm through his. "I like you!"

It's only when my dad laughs and says, "I like you too," that I realize it's been a long time since I've heard his laugh, and I've missed it quite a lot.

**

My dad offers to drive home and it feels good to sit in the passenger seat. To relax. To watch the familiar road from the other side, and to note people's mailboxes – some functional, some whimsical, and some falling apart. To let someone else remember the turn-offs and watch the speed limit. Although I still watch for deer. I can't stop doing that.

Once we merge onto the highway, he says, "So."

I look at him. There's less chance of a deer bounding in front of us now, so I can look away. "Yes. So."

"Was that what you meant by 'wait and see?'"

"I guess so." I'm not sure exactly what I meant, but there's nothing else I could have shown him, so that must have been it.

"Should I tell you what I saw?"

"If you think I can handle it." He'll probably think I'm joking – that's the idea – but there's an unsettling little churn in the pit of my stomach as I wait for him to answer.

"I've seen you win ribbons and trophies and medals, but today I saw something different." He pulls out to pass a slow-moving car, then adds, "Today I saw you doing something you liked and are good at. I haven't really seen that before."

"Oh," I say.

"What do you think about what I said?" he asks.

"I think you're probably right."

"What does that mean then?" he asks.

I straighten my seat belt, move the vents, then move them back. Adjust the sun visor. "I think it means, for now, I like things the way they are. I wouldn't really change anything."

"So, I can't gallop in and be Super-Dad by spending lots of money and buying you a new horse?"

I laugh. "I guess not." I look at him sideways. "But you could come out and see how it's going with Lucas sometimes."

He pulls back into the right lane. "I'd like that."

"And," I say, "If Laney ever decides to sell Lucas, I might end up asking Super-Dad for help then."

He touches his fingers to his forehead in a mock salute. "Super-Dad will be at attention in case that ever happens."

"Thanks," I say.

"Any time," he says. "That's what Super-Dads are for."

Chapter Thirty

"Your dad told me this is a busy week for you, getting ready for your riding workshop," my mom says. "I've shifted some things around so I can drive the boys to basketball this week."

I don't correct her and tell her it's a clinic, and I don't tell her since it's not a show I don't need to practice-till-perfect, and I could still spare the time to drive them. I say, "OK. Thanks," and I try to sound like it's all cool even though I had decided to finally do *something* to move things forward with Lucas. I thought maybe I'd buy tickets to the next basketball game at the university – four tickets, of course – and I'd ask Rory, and Ellie, and Lucas to come.

But I'd try to sit next to Lucas.

I had just about made up my mind to mention it casually, in the car, on the way to practice.

Now what?

Maybe my mom can ask for me ... I snort, and she asks, "What?"

"Nothing. Just you have to take the second entrance into the parking lot at St. Luke's because they're re-doing the bus turn-around."

"Thank you Mavis ... I mean, Em ... that was very nice of you to tell me."

"My pleasure," I say, trying not to think of courtside seats and me sitting next to Lucas, sharing a popcorn. I probably wouldn't have had the guts to ask anyway.

***

As it turns out, I need the extra time because my teachers have suddenly remembered they'll need to produce report cards soon, and have layered on the work. Between riding and school work I'm busier than I would have guessed.

The Bio lab I've been working on with Ellie is due Thursday. At lunch on Wednesday she finds me at my locker. "So, can we get together tonight to go over the report one more time?"

"The report's done," I tell her.

"I know, and it probably seems stupid, but I won't feel like it's *done*, done, until we read it through together."

This, I remember, is why I was happy to work with Ellie. She likes good marks, I like good marks, so I'm willing to humour her.

"Could we do it on the phone? After I get home from riding?"

She does that thing where her feet bounce, and her eyes sparkle, and she says, "That reminds me, can I come riding with you sometime?"

I tense. Ellie and I have been going along pretty well and I'm wondering if we're about to have an awkward moment. I would never dream of asking her if I could join her ringette practice (mostly because I'd fall on my butt), but lots of people seem to think you can snap your fingers and magic up a horse that they can ride with you.

I close my locker and turn to her. "Um, like, do you want to ride a horse?"

She laughs. "Wow! No. You must be so good, and I've never done it. But it would be fun to watch you ride."

I have a sudden image of Ellie sitting next to me in the passenger seat. Of Ellie talking a mile-a-minute about happy things – probably playing happy music. Of being able to show Lucas off to Ellie. I've been missing driving the guys to basketball. Having Ellie come riding with me might be a good substitute.

"Sure," I say. "If you really want to. But it might be boring, and your clothes could get dirty, and you'll definitely smell like horse after."

She shakes her head. "I won't be bored, and I'm guessing you've never smelled dirty ringette gear ... I can handle horse."

"Alright, then maybe on the weekend if there's a day you don't have ringette practice you can come with me?"

"Perfect!" she says. "And for tonight why don't you call me when you get home, and we'll go over the report together and make sure we're both happy and I'll submit it after we talk."

"Ellie?" I catch her just as she's about to turn away.

"Yeah?"

"Would you go to a basketball game at the university?"

She wrinkles her nose. "Don't you think we see enough basketball? There are these things called movies, and sometimes people even go shopping ... Oh, *wait*, do you mean a basketball game at the university not just with you?"

I nod.

"Like, maybe, you, and me, and Rory, and Lucas?"

"That was kind of the idea."

She swoops me up in a big hug. "That, is a brilliant idea! And I would so do it. What are the deets?"

"I, uh, I'll let you know. I just wanted to check if you were into it first."

She gives me a thumbs up. "Great! You snag the tickets and I'll pay you back for two of them." As she walks away she calls back over her shoulder. "The guys are going to love it!"

Which, yeah, she's probably right. As soon as I make a plan for asking Lucas.

**

The week passes by with all my assignments getting handed in on time, and me making endless lists of my absolute must-take items for the clinic, with notes at the bottom like, *Major tack scrubbing Friday night* and *Make sure grey breeches are clean.*

I tell myself I'm too busy to follow up on the basketball plans. Although I have bookmarked the university's home game schedule in my browser.

Most nights I can still squeeze a ride in before the sun goes down, but there's no mistaking the fall's taken hold. The other day I headed out to school past the sad frost-wilted remains of the annuals in my mom's flowerbeds which were still upright and flourishing just the day before. Digging my gloves out of the back of my tack locker is on my to-do list.

Friday night before the clinic I help Laney get the trailer ready before she goes to teach a lesson in the indoor arena, then I take Lucas out to the ring.

We don't have that much daylight left, but I don't really care. Tomorrow will be hard work, and lots of it. I have no intention of trying to learn anything new tonight. I just want to stretch out our riding muscles then bed Lucas down, fit, happy, and ready to go.

When I pull him up at the end of our short, simple ride his nostrils flare two clouds of breath into the crisp twilight air. The sky is layered with strips of burning-out sunlight, and gilded clouds.

I confront the stomach-fluttering, jaw-bone clenching, heart-quickening nerves that have been building all week and decide what happens tomorrow, at another barn, in another place, is unimportant as long as I have this to come back to.

"Same time, same place, next week?" I ask Lucas.

He snorts and gives his head a tiny shake, and I suck the near-night air into my lungs and say, "OK then. It's a date." Then, more quietly, to myself, "*Stonegate-Shmonegate ...*"

***

A headache's blooming and I'm freezing cold as we turn up the long maple-lined driveway. "Stonegate-Shmonegate."

"Pardon me?" Laney glances over but then looks straight back at the road so she can steer us smoothly around a deep pothole. *See? This place isn't perfect ...*

"I just ... nothing. Forget it. I'm getting a headache."

"Yeah? Well you're hunched over like a ninety-year-old who's done hard labour all her life, and if you keep frowning like that your face will stay that way, and let's just say it won't be an improvement."

I forgot it's No-Nonsense Laney in the truck with me. While I prefer funny, easy-going Laney, this Laney has been good for me – and for Lucas – more than once. Plus, I think she may be more able to deal with the stress of the day if she's not all soft-and-sweet.

Maybe I should revert to bitchy Mavis, too.

The vice grip on my brain intensifies. *I really, really need an ibuprofen.*

"Em!" Laney says. "Shoulders!"

I stick my tongue out at her, but after a second's pause I do straighten my shoulders. Then I roll them back, one at a time.

The pain in my head moderates.

"Now that face," Laney says. "Smile. Even if it's fake. Just do it."

My smile, phony as it is, loosens my jaw, stretches my cheeks, and eases the tug across my forehead.

OK. Fine. Maybe I won't go full-on Mavis. Maybe not just yet. I'll reserve judgment, I won't go Ellie-happy, but for now I'll stay quietly Em-like.

Chapter
Thirty-One

If there was one symbol of everything that went wrong for me at Stonegate, it was Grace. Grace, who was the polar opposite of me.

Where I was a completely ineffective rider, with a very expensive horse to keep me in the ribbons, Grace was an amazing, adaptive, creative rider, who could take horses nobody else could even ride, and win on them.

Grace was also naturally pretty, naturally charming, naturally likeable.

People and horses are drawn to her.

All this made me very, very, very insecure around Grace.

Which made me act very badly.

Which is one of the reasons I had to leave Stonegate quick-in-a-hurry before Drew actually gave my stall to somebody else.

All of which, now, I'm pretty embarrassed about.

Grace is in my group.

Of course she is.

After the half-dozen of us have all successfully walk-trotted – "successful" meaning nobody collides with anybody else – Laney calls us in to stand in a half-circle facing her and asks each one of us to introduce ourselves, say why we're here, and what we hope to accomplish.

When it's her turn, Grace runs her hand down her gelding's neck – Sprite: the horse who was sold once, and had to be returned to Stonegate because Grace was the only person who could handle him – and smiles and says, "He's very brave, and goey, and I think eventing would suit him." Then, with a sweet laugh, she adds, "And dressage is our huge weak point, as everybody will see before long."

While I'm sure Grace genuinely thinks dressage is her weak point and, knowing Sprite, it's not something that would come naturally to him, I'm still pretty sure she's going to put in a lovely, capable performance and make the rest of us, who are truly struggling, feel like crap. That's just what Grace does.

When Laney turns to me, I'm flummoxed. In a way, I feel like I don't count. I'm Laney's token participant. But I registered, and my dad wrote a cheque (although Laney trailered Lucas over here for free) so I guess I get the full experience.

Not that I really want it.

"I, uh ..." and then it all gets complicated, because there's at least one additional girl – other than Grace – who knew me as "Mavis" and even though I'm used to being "Em" now, this particular situation is weird.

Laney helps, by saying, "Yes, Em, go ahead," so I say, "I'm Em, and this is Lucas, and we're aiming to compete in our first, very small, event in the spring, and this clinic seems like a good stepping-stone."

Nobody falls off their horse when I say my name's "Em," – although I'm not facing Grace at the moment, so who knows how she reacts – then Laney claps her hands together and says, "OK, based on what you all said, here's what I propose we work on today ..." and we begin work, which is great because it distracts me from all my possible sources of nerves. Which are:

1) Lucas. Now settled at home, part of me was definitely afraid he'd be frazzled and uncontrollable off the premises. This, though, is where the solid part of Lucas's personality shows through. Initially I thought a trail horse would be lazy and slow. I was wrong about that. He is, however, unflappable and unconcerned by the world around him. Every now and then he sighs, and I scratch his withers, and of course, he has the familiarity of Laney in the middle of the ring, so our only issues are the normal ones we'd face in any ride. Which leads to concern number two:

2) Me. Us. We will not be good enough. We won't keep up. Everybody else will ride circles around us. It's just not the case. Each person in this ring has strengths, and each has weaknesses. One woman has a huge amount of trouble getting her horse to step forward. Another is plank-stiff on the left rein. One won't take the left lead canter – and I know how frustrating that can be – and Grace, even perfect Grace, is ... well ... not perfect. She and Sprite are having big issues with accuracy, and being inaccurate is a quick and avoidable way to lose points. Sprite is smart, no doubt about it, and I watch many times as Grace asks him to do something once, then the next time through he remembers and decides to do it again, before she can ask, twenty feet too soon. "Aarrgghh!" Grace says, and for the first time ever, I feel her pain completely and thoroughly.

"Take a break!" Laney tells her, and as Grace peels off, it just so happens Sprite falls into a walk next to Lucas and me.

Grace reaches under the pommel to free a hunk of Sprite's mane and tells him, "You are such a pain."

This is awkward. This is hard. This is intimidating. *I can do this.* "He looks really good," I tell her.

She looks at me sideways, and waits, as though I might add something at the end, like 'For a crazy horse,' or 'Too bad he doesn't *act* good.' When I don't, she says, "It's never easy with him. Ever."

I wonder if that's a dig at me for my history of riding pushbutton horses who, let's face it, were always easy. Always. For that matter, she has no idea how much work I've done with Lucas. Maybe she thinks he's a perfectly trained horse whose mistakes only come from my terrible riding.

It's tempting to lash out, or to explain. Instead I say, "I've started trying this thing, when my ride goes sideways. I start over with my warm-up. Maybe not even a full warm-up, but just something to break the pattern."

Again, a double blink before she replies, then she says, "That's probably exactly what I should be doing. We both need a reset."

I have no way of knowing if she peels off on a small circle because she genuinely wants to re-start her warm-up on Sprite, or if it was just a good excuse to get away from me, but at least that encounter wasn't a disaster. I handled it. It was OK.

3) Then there's my third major worry. Facing my old coach – Drew – who knows me as an unfit, unmotivated, barely coachable rider who didn't progress at all while he taught me and who often lashed out at him, the other riders in my lesson, and – possibly worst of all – my horse.

The main source of Laney's nerves about today was building a relationship with Stonegate. What would they think of her clinic? Would they be able to set up some kind of partnership? There's no doubt Drew will stroll over to watch her teach.

Which means he'll watch me ride.

Right before we break for lunch, Laney gives us a mini-test to ride. "We'll concentrate on walk-trot-halt in this one," she says. "There will be circles, and a change of rein across the diagonal, and I'll give a canter option at the end if you feel like your horse is balanced, and it will work for you. Mostly, I'll be looking for general ease of going, and accuracy." Grace's sigh travels across the row of waiting riders.

Laney reads out the test and I think she's going to send me out first, but Grace speaks up. "Could we just do it now, so he can't watch anyone else and figure it out?"

She goes, and the accuracy is quite good. Grace and Sprite have always been a nice pair, but they've also always competed in the jumper ring, where it's all about rails left up and time elapsed, and it doesn't matter how they look. Here, in their early days of dressage, it's clear they're going to need to work together to look less rushed; more at ease.

As Grace is finishing, Drew comes and leans on the fence and I have a *Gre-e-eat* moment, because I know I'm next and he's watching.

Sure enough, Laney nods me forward. Before I take my first step, Laney looks straight at me and does this thing where she blows her cheeks up big and chipmunky, then lets the air out, and I think, *OK, yeah – breathe,* and I do, and it makes everything much, much better.

Essentially our test is about decision-making and priorities. I weight the overall impact of the ride over the individual components so, a couple of times, *yes,* I could have had a quicker, sharper transition, but, *yes,* Lucas would also have tensed, and run, and I would have tensed right back, so it's worth it to be half-a-beat off. To overrun our mark by a few feet.

I feel good and he feels good. Maybe too good.

"If you're up to it, canter at 'C'!" Laney calls.

Drew's watching, and Grace is watching, and I have a lot to prove, so of course I'm up to it. I exhale, line up my aids, given them all at once, and am – just perhaps – a little too clear. A smidge too definite.

Lucas bucks. A huge buck and strangely – fleetingly – it goes through my mind that if I were watching it, instead of sitting it, it might be a very beautiful buck.

I jam my heels down, and focus on keeping my hands steady and, apparently, the buck had nothing to do with bad temper, and there's no grudge, because he lands on the correct lead, in a forward canter, and carries himself through a sweeping circle.

In a horse show, that would have just cost me the class.

Which is why it's weird that I feel like this clinic wouldn't have been the same without it.

It's only as I resume my spot parallel to the fence that I remember Drew.

Oh.

Drew, just possibly, might not have found the buck as unique a mark of charming individuality as I did.

He's tailing off a sentence to Laney, "... always did have good hands."

Me?!?

No way. He can't be talking about me, can he? He must mean the next rider.

But I glance up to see who's going next and – without being nasty – it's safe to say her hands are not her strong point. She has good leg position, but even as I watch, she reefs her horse in the mouth.

Could he mean me? Could I have had one, small, redeeming feature when I rode here?

I'll have to ask Laney on the way home.

Chapter
Thirty-Two

Today was important to Laney, I know that, so I take the fact that Drew is having a long chat with her as a good sign, and I get on with loading the trailer.

Like so much in my riding life, nobody ever taught me to do this, but I've seen other people doing it enough to know what has to be done. The difference now, with Lucas, is I take that initiative.

First, I straighten the tack area; making sure everything's secure and not likely to get flung around on the journey. Since I have time, I wipe down my tack now so I can just slide it away once we get home.

Next, I get the traveling area of the trailer neat and tidy, and ready for Lucas. Including, of course, a nicely filled hay net.

I prepare Lucas last – the sweat marks from under his saddle are long-since dry in the crisp fall air, and after I've brushed him there's no indication left that he was even ridden today. While he pulls at the hay net I snug his legs into long, thick shipping bandages.

I stand back and survey the results. Clean, travel-ready horse. Belongings and trailer ship-shape.

This time last year I would have waited for somebody else to come along and do these things for me and it wouldn't only have been because I was lazy, or thought I was too good to do them – although that's probably how it looked. There was also the fact that I would have doubted my ability. Would have figured someone else knew better than me.

These days I figure nobody knows Lucas better than me, so I might as well get on with it.

"Wow! It looks like you have everything under control!" Laney arrives just as I've settled Lucas in the trailer. She helps me lift the ramp and secure it, then brushes her hands on her thighs. "Ready to go?"

"Do you want to check anything over, first?" I ask.

She furrows her brow, frowns, "Uh, nope. If you did it, that's good with me."

"I ... uh ... OK ..." I swing into the passenger seat and wonder if it's weird that I feel more pride in sorting out the trailer than I did in my ride in the clinic – although that was good, too.

"We'll have to teach you to haul the trailer," Laney says. "Then I can sit back and drink coffee on the way home from events."

"That would be great," I say. And I mean it.

As we crawl back out the long lane, we pass Sprite, head down, tearing at the normally out-of-bounds lush green grass that grows between the paddock fences and the driveway. Grace, holding his lead, looks up. She hesitates for only the smallest of seconds, then lifts her hand. I lift mine back and she nods.

It's not best-friends-forever, and it's nothing worthy of the Nobel Peace Prize, but it's a million times better than I could have ever imagined we'd achieve. I'm good with it.

We pick up speed on the main road, and I turn to Laney. "So?"

She nods, like she's confirming something. "So, yeah. So, the other riders told me they liked the clinic, and a couple of them told Drew they liked it, too. Which means he's happy."

"And what does that mean?" I ask.

She exhales her breath in an audible puff. "I guess it means options, possibilities. It means maybe working together in the future. He also told me if I ever wanted to move over and coach at Stonegate, we could talk about it."

Oh ... "Oh," I say. "I'd miss you."

"Well, you could come."

"I'm not so sure about that."

"Em!" That warning note jumps really quickly into Laney's voice, and I've learned not to ignore it.

"What?"

"You did great today. And it all went fine, right?"

Fine? Yes. Perfect? No. But I wasn't expecting perfect. "Yes."

"Drew liked Lucas, and he liked the way you rode him ..."

This is the moment to ask what, exactly, Drew said about my hands. I consider how to word it – how to ask without sounding conceited, or desperate – then I think maybe, instead, I should ask another question now. Ask about Sasha's statement that Laney tricked me into liking Lucas. This could be the time to get that out in the open.

Or ...

I remember what Laney said when we were talking about me registering in the clinic – "... the important thing is, I'm glad I gave you a chance," she said. "So just focus on that; it doesn't really matter what happened before, or exactly how we got here, we're here and it's all good."

We're here and it's all good ... is that true?

Because if that's true it doesn't matter what Drew used to think about my hands, or whether Laney had a plan to get me to like Lucas. It just matters what's happening right now, and what could happen tomorrow.

I keep quiet and, like a gift for my restraint, Laney offers me some information: "Drew specifically mentioned the improvement he saw in you."

I snort. "Ha! Because I had lots of room for improvement, right?"

But secretly, quietly, I'm happy. I'll take it. It's a step forward.

As we pull into our own familiar drive, and to the stable yard that's come to feel like home, I circle back to our earlier discussion. "So, about moving to Stonegate, that's not a *plan* right now, is it?"

Laney ease the truck to a smooth stop, then turns to me. "Honestly? I've been pretty happy with the way things are going around here, so my plan is to just keep doing what we've been doing. For now. How does that plan sound to you?"

I think of my conversation with my dad. Think of how I told him I don't want to change anything. "It sounds good to me. For now."

"Great!" Laney slides the keys out of the ignition. "And it's always nice to know people like what you're doing, and that you have options, so enjoy that feeling, but enjoy it while you put your horse away!"

Chapter Thirty-Three

Lucas's coat is already thickening so I can press my palm into it and the outline stays for a second. Laney and I have been talking about how to approach the winter – will we blanket him? Will we let his coat grow and clip him? She's thinking of trying to keep a sand ring plowed so we can ride outside where he'll be less likely to overheat than in the indoor arena.

It's fun to talk to her about all the possibilities. Fun to be consulted like an equal. Fun to make plans.

It's been dark for a while when I get home, yet there's a figure taking shots at our basketball net.

And that figure is not my brother.

I pull the car well up the driveway to keep it out of stray ball territory, and step out of the car. The evening air bites. There's frost most nights now and it's descending already. I hug my arms tight across the front of me.

Lucas has stopped and is holding the ball against his hip. "What're you doing here?" I ask.

"Came to shoot some hoops with my favourite baller," he says.

"So, where is my brother?"

He doesn't answer, just bounces the ball at me. I automatically uncross my arms and reach for it. After that the dribble comes naturally. Forward, forward, until Lucas is blocking my way, then pull up and shoot.

He retrieves the rebound, and I ask again. "Where's Rory?"

Lucas shrugs and heads for the basket. I stand and watch, and he slows and says, "That all you got?"

At the last minute, I bolt forward and knock the ball out of his hand as he shoots it. "Hey! Goaltending!" he says.

"Yeah, whatever. Maybe I'd fall for that if I hadn't read the rulebook. Besides, you've got half-a-foot on me – I can do anything I need to keep up."

"Oh, it's like that, is it?" He grabs the ball from in front of me. "Fine. Game on."

I heat up fast, shucking my long-sleeved top off so I'm running, dribbling, shooting, playing in a tank top and breeches. Not exactly near-November clothes but, then again, Lucas is in shorts.

I don't tire out, though. Running has given me an internal rhythm. It helps me keep up with Lucas. I'm not saying I make it hard on him, but he's getting a work-out too – he's breathing hard, and the streetlights catch the glisten of sweat around his hairline.

We end up in a wrestle over the ball and, true to my word of doing anything I can to keep up, I snake my foot around his ankle and trip him. Except, that means tripping myself, too, since I go down with the falling ball.

We land half on the lawn, legs on the driveway and, for a few seconds the world keeps spinning even though we've stopped moving.

The black sky, and the spray of stars, and the sliver of moon, all whirling above us, make me feel tiny, then it's Lucas, tall, strong, and radiating body heat in contrast to the cold grass, that makes me feel small.

I start to scramble to my feet, but Lucas won't let go of the ball, and for some reason it doesn't occur to me that I can just release it, so I stay lying beside him, ribs heaving.

He puts his hand on my ribcage – spreading his fingers wide, the way he does to span a basketball – and the shock jolts me. Both shocks, because there's the surprise that he's doing this – touching me – layered on top of the deep physical bolt of sensation, of butterflies in my stomach, and tightness in my core, and giddiness in my head.

I remember I can let go of the ball, and I lift my hand and touch his cheek, and he squeezes my side, and pulls me as close as he can, with a great big basketball stuck between us.

It's close enough, though, for his mouth to reach mine. He brushes his lips sideways across mine and it's like little sparks going off, one after the other, all along my mouth, and then we're kissing, properly, and finally he mumbles, "Friggin' basketball," and flips it out of the way and our bodies push against each other.

"I'm sweaty," I whisper.

"Join the club," he says, and nips at my sweaty neck and some kind of circuit of pleasure trips in my brain.

"I smell like horse."

"You smell like you."

I press my palm flat against his – yes – sweaty shirt and between kisses I mumble, "I like you."

"Mmm," he says. "Good thing or I'd wonder about your judgment rolling around on your parents' front lawn kissing me."

"I do this most Wednesdays," I say.

"If I'd known, I'd have started coming over on Wednesdays a long time ago."

He shifts his weight on top of me and it feels good, but it also feels reassuring. Like he'll protect me from anything. Including my neighbour's headlights sweeping over us.

"Whoops," I say. "Maybe we should go inside."

***

"Hot chocolate?" I ask.

"Yes, please."

I get mugs, and I get milk, and hot chocolate mix and I manage it all because I don't look at him.

"With marshmallows?" I ask.

"Oh, baby," he says, and that makes me laugh, and look at him, and then I'm sunk.

I don't remember where the marshmallows are. Can't remember if we even have marshmallows. Can't figure out where to start looking.

I just stare at Lucas, and I'm holding the hot chocolate tin, and I'm accomplishing absolutely nothing, and he's staring at me, and we're both grinning, and that's all fine until Rory walks in.

"Hey!" he says. "Hot chocolate – excellent – make me one, Sis?"

"Huh? What?"

Rory snaps his fingers in front of my eyes and I look down at the tin. "Oh, yeah. OK."

"Tonight?" Rory asks. "Is that possible?"

"I, uh … can you remind me if we have marshmallows?"

"What is up with you?" he asks.

I look at Lucas and, even though I try not to smile, my heart beats faster, and my cheeks warm. Rory follows my gaze to Lucas, who also has two bright spots on his cheeks, and my brother groans. "No …"

"Sorry, dude," Lucas says.

Rory shrugs. "I guess it had to happen. I guess it's not the end of the world – you'll probably get sick of her soon." Then he takes the tin out of my hands. "How about I make the hot chocolate, so we might actually get to drink it tonight?"

"Thanks," Lucas and I say it at the same time.

"Jinx!" We say in unison, then we giggle.

"Oh, Lord help me," Rory mutters as he yanks a bag of marshmallows out of the cupboard.

Chapter
Thirty-Four

I knew it would be great sitting next to Lucas at the university basketball game, and it is. We share Twizzlers, and we bump shoulders, and every now and then he laces his fingers through mine and squeezes and – *oooh* ... everything in me flutters.

But what makes it even better is that Ellie is on my other side. And Rory's on the other side of her.

The music pumps and the baskets swish. The cheerleaders throw out t-shirts and Rory catches one – which is just as well, because it's an XXL so neither Ellie nor I could wear it.

At half-time Ellie and I wait in the bathroom line-up together and she nudges me and says, "Hey, what did you think of number seven on the Bio test today?"

"You mean the one where you couldn't tell if the line was pointing to the nucleus or if it was supposed to be in the cytoplasm?"

"*Yes!* Exactly! It drives me crazy when he puts stuff like that on his tests. I swear, if I lose a mark over that ..."

I clap my hand over my mouth and suck my breath in, and Ellie says, "What? What is it Em?"

For a second my eyes are watery, and I blink them twice. Because not only is this conversation not irritating me – I'll happily rehash it all over again with Ellie when we get the test back. That's what friends are for.

A door opens and a mom leads her small daughter out and over to the sink, and I point Ellie toward the empty stall. "It's nothing. I'm fine. You go ahead."

"No, you," she says.

"Nope," I say. "I insist. Friends first."

***

Later in the fall, there's a single weekend in Toronto when Ellie has a ringette tournament, Rory and Lucas have a basketball tournament, and the Royal Winter Fair is on.

The tournament schedules keep me from going to the big evening horse show at the Royal, but I get over there for a couple of hours in the day. It's long enough for me to buy a funky pair of riding socks, and a new halter for Lucas, as well as a pretty horseshoe necklace I think Laney will like.

I catch some of the Hunter division and, lo and behold, I just happen to be watching when Ava comes into the ring.

She looks great. With Lucas's coat coming in thick enough for small mammals to nest in, I've almost forgotten how shiny a horse can be. Ava gleams. Her paces are perfect and she carries herself and her sweet new rider beautifully. At the end of her flawless round, her owner reaches down and scratches her withers and Ava's ears flick back to her.

I recognize the reaction because now I've had a horse react that way to me. Ava loves her rider.

Which is great.

I'm happy for them for finding each other.

I'm happy for my parents for riding out my dad's absence and getting to be back together.

I'm happy for Rory and Ellie who are even stronger since Rory, unfortunately, had his first seizure in ages, and Ellie was right there with him the whole time. That's what my brother deserves.

And it's easy for me to be happy for them because of everything I have, including my two Lucases.

I have just enough time to wait through the apple dumpling line at the Royal, order half-a-dozen to go, then head out to catch a taxi to the downtown gym where I'll meet my mom, and Ellie, and we'll watch Rory and Lucas, and everyone can have an apple dumpling.

PLEASE LEAVE A REVIEW!

Reviews help me sell books. More sales let me write more books. A simple star rating and a few quick words are all that's needed to help other readers evaluate my books and, hopefully, buy them!

To review on **Amazon**, please follow this link – https://tinyurl.com/TudorAmazon – and select the book you want to review.

To review on **Goodreads**, this is the link – https://tinyurl.com/TudorGoodreads.

If you liked this book ...

... you might enjoy Tudor's other books. Read the first chapter of *Appaloosa Summer*, the first book in the Island Series, to find out.

Chapter One

Appaloosa Summer • Island Series
Book One

I'm staring down a line of jumps that should scare my brand-new show breeches right off me.

But it doesn't. Major and I know our jobs here. His is to read the combination, determine the perfect take-off spot, and adjust his stride accordingly. Mine is to stay out of his way and let him jump.

We hit the first jump just right. He clears it with an effortless arc, and all I have to do is go through my mental checklist. Heels down. Back straight. Follow his mouth.

"Good boy, Major." One ear flicks halfway back to acknowledge my comment, but not enough to make him lose focus. A strong, easy stride to jump two, and he's up, working for both of us, holding me perfectly balanced as we fly through the air.

He lands with extra momentum; normal at the end of a long, straight line. He self-corrects, shifting his weight back over his hocks. Next will come the surge from his muscled hind end; powering us both up, and over, the final tall vertical.

It doesn't come, though. How can it not? "Come on!" I cluck, scuff my heels along his side. No response from my rock-solid jumper.

The rails are right in front of us, but I have no horse-power – nothing – under me. By the time I think of going for my stick, it's too late. We slam into several closely spaced rails topping a solid gate. Oh God. Oh no. Be ready, be ready, be ready. But how? There's no good way. There are poles everywhere, and leather tangling, and dirt. In my eyes, in my nose, in my mouth.

There's no sound from my horse. Is he as winded as me? I can't speak, or yell, or scream. Major? Is that him on my leg? Is that why it's numb? People come, kneel around me. I can't see past them. I can't sit up. My ears rush and my head spins. I'm going to throw up. "I'm going to …"

**

I flush the toilet. Swish out my mouth. Avoid looking in the mirror. Light hurts, my reflection hurts, everything hurts at this point in the afternoon, when the headache builds to its peak.

Why me?

I've never lost anybody close to me. My grandpa died before I was born, and my widowed grandma's still going strong at ninety-four. She has an eighty-nine-year-old boyfriend. They go to the racetrack; play the slots.

If I had to predict who would die first in my life, I would never, in a million years, have guessed it would be my fit, young, strong thoroughbred.

Never.

But he did.

Thinking about it just sharpens the headache, so I press a towel against my face, blink into the soft fluffiness.

"Are you OK?" Slate's voice comes through the door. With my mom and dad at work, Slate's been the one to spend the last three days distracting me when I'm awake, and waking me up whenever I get into a sound sleep. Or that's what it feels like.

"Fine." I push the bathroom door open.

"Puke?"

I nod. Stupid move. It hurts. Whisper instead. "Yes."

"Well, that's a big improvement. Just the once today."

She follows me back to my room. She's not a pillow-plumper or quilt-smoother – I have to struggle into my rumpled bed – but it's nice to have her around. "I'm glad you're here, Slatey." I sniffle, and taste salt in the back of my throat.

I'm close to tears all the time these days. "Normal," the doctor said. Apparently, tears aren't unreasonable after suffering a knock to the head hard enough to split my helmet in two, with my horse dropping stone cold dead underneath me in the show ring. I'm still sick of crying, though. And puking, too.

"Don't be stupid, Meg; being here is heaven. My mom and Agate are going completely over the top organizing Aggie's sweet sixteen. There are party planning boards everywhere, and her dance friends are always over giggling about it too."

"Just as long as it's not about me. I don't want to owe you."

"'Course not; you're not that great of a best friend."

***

The way I know I've fallen asleep again, is that Slate is shaking me awake. Again.

"Huh?" I open one eye. Squinting. The sunlight doesn't hurt. In fact, it feels kind of nice. I open both eyes.

"Craig's here."

I struggle to get my elbows under me, and the shot of pain to my head tells me I've moved too fast.

"Craig?"

She's nodding, eyes wide.

"Like our Craig?"

"Uh-huh."

First my mom canceled her business trip scheduled for the day after the accident; now our eighty-dollar-an-hour, Level Three riding coach is at my house. "Are you sure I'm not dying, and you just haven't told me?"

"I was wondering the same thing."

"What am I wearing?" I blink at cropped yoga pants and a t-shirt I got in a 10K race pack. It doesn't really matter – I've never seen Craig when I'm not wearing breeches and boots; never seen, or even imagined him in the city – changing clothes is hardly going to make a difference.

Slate leads the way down the stairs, through the hallway and into the kitchen, where Craig's shifting from foot to foot, reading the calendar on the fridge. He must be bored if he wants the details of my dad's Open Houses, my mom's travel itinerary.

"Smoking," Slate whispers just before Craig turns to me. And, technically, she's right. His eyes are just the right shade of emerald, surrounded by lashes long enough to be appealing, while stopping short of girly. His cheekbones are high and pronounced, just like his jawbone. And his broad, tan shoulders, and the narrow hips holding up his broken-in jeans are the natural trademarks of somebody who works hard – mostly outside – for a living.

But he's our riding coach. Craig, and our fifty-five-year-old obese vice-principal (with halitosis), are the two men in the world Slate won't flirt with. I don't flirt with him, mostly because I've never met a guy I like more than my horse. Major ...

"Hey Meg." Craig's quiet voice is a first. The gentle hug. He steps back, eyes searching my head. "Do you have a bump?"

I take a deep breath and throw my shoulders back. "Nope." Knock my knuckles on my temple. "All the damage is internal."

Craig's brow furrows. "Meg, you can tell me how you really feel." No I can't. Of course I can't. Even if I could explain the emptiness of losing my three-hour-a-day, seven-day-a-week companion, the guilt at "saving" him from the racetrack only to kill him in the jumper ring, and the take-it-or-leave-it feeling I have about showing again, none of that is conversation for a sunny springtime afternoon.

Still, I can offer a bit of show and tell. "I have tonnes of bruises. And I've puked every day so far. And, this is weird but, look." I use my index finger to push my earlobe forward. "My earring caught on something and tore right through."

The colour drains from Craig's face, and now I think he might puke.

"Meg!" Slate pokes me in the back. "Sit down with Craig and I'll make tea."

Craig pulls something out of his pocket, places it on the table. A brass plate reading **Major**. The one from his stall door. "We have the rest of his things in the tack room. We put them all together for you."

Yeah, because you wanted to rent out the stall. I can't blame him. There's a massive waiting list to train with Craig. And my horse had the consideration to die right at the beginning of the show season. Some new boarder had her summer dream come true.

I reach out; turn the plaque around to face me. Craig's trained me too well – tears in one of his lessons result in a dismissal from the ring – so now, even with a concussion, I can't cry in front of him. Deep breath. I rub my thumb over the engraved letters M-A-J-O-R. "There was nothing that horse couldn't do."

Craig sighs. "You're right. He was one in a million. Have you thought about replacing him?"

If you liked the first chapter of Appaloosa Summer, why not read the rest of the book? Appaloosa Summer is available as an eBook or paperback on Amazon.

ABOUT THE AUTHOR

Tudor Robins is the author of books that move – she wants to move your heart, mind, and pulse with her writing. Tudor lives in Ottawa, Canada, and when she's not writing she loves horseback riding, running, being outdoors, and spending time with her family.

Tudor would love to hear from you at
tudor@tudorrobins.ca .

Printed in Great Britain
by Amazon